# GOOD DAY?

VESNA MAIN was born in Zagreb, Croatia. She studied comparative literature before obtaining a doctorate from the Shakespeare Institute in Birmingham. She has worked as a journalist, lecturer and teacher. Her two novels are *A Woman With No Clothes On* (Delancey Press, 2008) and *The Reader the Writer* (Mirador, 2015). The latter is written entirely in dialogue and one of the characters is a young prostitute who is also the protagonist of 'Safe'. Recent short stories have appeared in *Persimmon Tree* and *Winamop*.

Also by Vesna Main

# GOOD DAY?

## VESNA MAIN

SALT

CROMER

PUBLISHED BY SALT PUBLISHING 2019

2 4 6 8 10 9 7 5 3 1

First published in Great Britain in 2019 by
Salt Publishing Ltd
International House, 24 Holborn Viaduct, London EC1A 2BN United Kingdom

www.saltpublishing.com

Salt Publishing Limited Reg. No. 5293401

A CIP catalogue record for this book is available from the British Library

ISBN 978 1 78463 191 8 (Paperback edition)
ISBN 978 1 78463 192 5 (Electronic edition)

Typeset in Neacademia by Salt Publishing

A

*for* Peter

§

- Good day?
- Fine, thanks. And you?
- Not bad. What did Anna get up to today?
- I thought you didn't like her.
- She's a difficult woman.
- There would be no point if she were perfect.
- Perfect? I can hardly find anything to like about her.
- She's clever—
- Academically clever, I give you that, but not in other ways.
- You're too harsh. She's artistic—
- So what?
- She has a great figure, lots of friends.
- Good for her.
- She's an excellent cook.
- I'll take your word for that.
- She's passionate about things that matter: love, art, books, friendships—
- Because those are things that matter to you.
- Aren't they important to you?
- Yes, but not in that order.
- Okay, not in that order.
- There is also kindness, social justice . . .
- I hope so. One little difference between you and Anna.
- You're wrong.
- Tell me.

I

- I don't know everything about her but I'm sure she would care about social justice.
- She might try putting it into practice once in a while.
- No snide remarks, please. She's a warm person. Okay, if you asked her what she cared about, kindness wouldn't necessarily be the first thing that came to her mind.
- Evidently not.
- I think I have to come up with something to make her less wonderful.
- You must be joking. You mean apart from the fact that she's opinionated, pretentious, controlling and that she has a temper.
- Are you trying to justify what he did by making her out to be bad?
- Not at all.
- You're supporting the man by rubbishing the woman.
- I think it would help the novel if the reader liked her, cared—
- I don't think in such terms. That's not what novels are about.
- Of course they are. Even a serial murderer has to have something to make the reader care.
- I think the reader would like Anna.
- You like her because she's similar to you.
- She is not me.
- I'm not sure of that.
- I see. Are you trying to say you don't like me?
- Don't be silly. I'm talking about Anna. People wouldn't think much of her.
- But why? What's wrong with her? Give me a specific example.

- The way she reacts is completely over the top.
- What's over the top when something like that happens?
- What she does is over the top.
- Someone else might have killed him, certainly thrown him out.
- Possibly, but the way she goes on and on, she might just as well have done.
- She can't simply forget it. It's not a broken plate, or even a crashed car.
- After a while she should draw a line. Move on. Make an effort.
- Make an effort, like he did. Lots of effort over eight years.
- Sometimes you sound like her: harping on about the same thing. And like her, you're looking back, always looking back. That's what's so irritating about her—
- You're talking about me.
- No. I'm saying that she always wants to blame. She's not interested in finding a solution.
- It's a big thing. The most tragic event in her life. She can't help looking back.
- Come on. People getting cancer, losing a loved one, that's tragic, not what Richard—
- You can always find someone worse off.
- You ought to see that Anna is an unsympathetic character.
- I disagree.
- You have made her too much in your own image.
- That's what I said: You think Anna is like me and you don't like Anna.
- No, I didn't mean that. I was making two different points. Anyway, she isn't quite like you but she has some of your faults.

- Some? You mean I have more than her?
- I didn't say that. Look, don't take it personally.
- It's frustrating when you take a male position.
- What else can I do?
- See how she feels.
- Like you see how he feels?
- I do. But he's the guilty party.
- It's not that simple. She's not the easiest of people—
- So, what he did is her fault?
- I didn't say that.
- But you implied it.
- I'm trying to be helpful. Didn't even Sarah find Anna's reaction over the top?
- No, but she disapproves of what Anna does later.
- Obviously. Why can't you see it? Proves my point: even the few sympathetic readers would abandon her when she won't let go.
- I want the reader to understand how difficult it is for Anna. She knows what she is doing and she hates herself for that.
- Really?
- Yes, she understands that she is compromising her feminist politics.
- That's crap. She obviously never really felt that; she's just posing.
- Not at all. She was forced into that position. All because of him. She hates him for doing that to her.
- Self-indulgence.
- She's feeling low. She's been rejected.
- She hasn't. At no point does Richard reject her.
- That's what it feels like.

- But he never walked out on her. He never stopped loving her.
- Maybe not but the way she feels, she needs to seek approbation. Male approbation.
- She gets it from her first blind date—
- Not really. A boring, unattractive lawyer pontificating about wine is hardly going to make her feel desired.
- Why does she agree to meet him in a hotel then?
- It's her first blind date. Her first ever. Doesn't know how to let him down.
- She doesn't strike me as unassertive.
- True but she's sensitive as well. She tries to help when he loses his erection. When it doesn't work, she thinks he doesn't find her attractive. In a different way, she feels rejected again.
- Well, she could have had that builder from *Time Out*: twenty-five, 'with a big one'. Didn't he promise her she wouldn't be disappointed?
- What a male mind you have.
- What else am I supposed to have?
- You know what I mean. Women don't think like that. A big one. Rubbish. What she needs is to be desired, desired as a woman.
- Except by a builder. And he even rang her back. And again. When do you get a builder who does that? Ring you back.
- Not often.
- But Anna's a snob. She wouldn't meet him because she didn't think he'd read Beckett. Didn't she make some comment about being worried what they would talk about? Talk about? They would fuck.
- Don't be so crude. Anna needs more than that.

- What? Five men on the go?
- They complement one another.
- She's hypocritical. She claims to worry about what she's doing to their marriages, allegedly being all feminist and sisterly but carrying on anyway.
- She's trying to help herself. He destroyed her confidence as a woman.
- Helping herself at the expense of other women?
- That bothers her, I've just told you.
- If she wanted to help herself, she should have stayed with the therapist. Or wasn't that as much fun?
- The sessions were unhelpful.
- She couldn't face the therapist saying that in relationships things are never one-sided and that she—
- Don't tell me again that she drove him to—
- She bears some responsibility for what happened.
- No. He chose to act as he did. It had nothing to do with her.
- Yes. She chose to act as she did. It had nothing to do with him.
- That's disingenuous.
- In relationships it's never only one to blame.
- It is in this case.
- It wasn't easy for him.
- What do you mean? Living with an intelligent, attractive woman, good at organising suppers with friends.
- That supper, my goodness, really shows her—
- As a great host, a kind friend, an articulate woman.
- She only organises the dinner to control everybody.
- I know what goes on in her mind, not you.
- I do too; I've read the chapter. You forget it's all an internal

monologue; it's easy to know what she thinks.

- When you invite friends around, you want everything to go smoothly; you want everyone to enjoy themselves.
- Not Anna. She just wants to pull the strings. They're all her puppets. Do you remember how she objects when Mark moves the candlestick from one part of the table to another; she worries that he has made it too symmetric.
- She cares what things look like; she doesn't like symmetry. But she doesn't tell him off.
- Well, she moves the candlestick back. Probably ostentatiously, making a point. And her thoughts on where the flowers should be, the glasses, the cutlery, and goodness knows what else.
- You're terribly unfair.
- She's preoccupied with her own obsessions; doesn't give a toss about anyone else.
- You have no visual sense; you can't understand how she feels. To some of us, such things matter. Anna is particular about details: laying the table for her guests is one of them.
- A nice moment of irony in that chapter.
- ?
- When you make her think that Richard cares about the way the table is laid and that he insists on doing it himself and when he's late and she has to do it, she worries that he would complain. He couldn't care less. Shows how little she knows him after twenty-five years of marriage.
- Not her fault; he's never told her. Richard's not the most outspoken person.
- Difficult to get a word in with a woman like that.
- For you, everything wrong with him is her fault. She's a lovely person.

7

- Is that the same person who thinks all those disparaging thoughts about people she invited to dinner and who is critical of anyone who isn't like her? As Richard says—
- Are you quoting him?
- Why not? I agree with him when he says some people are more relaxed and let things happen at parties. Anna doesn't. You don't. But the world is different. The two of you can't take it.
- Don't make it personal. It's not about me.
- She invites her friends and then shows no empathy. It's as if they're all there for her indulgence. And Sarah - by the way, why did you call her Sarah? - she's right to say that Anna is playing Mrs Dalloway.
- Well, at that point, Sarah—
- Why did you call her Sarah?
- A tribute to my best friend. Sarah doesn't mind.
- I'm surprised. As for Anna, there's also that time in the kitchen, when they're getting the dessert out and Mark talks about his depression and inability to paint and all she can say is 'paint black'.
- Good advice.
- Shows her complete lack of understanding. For all her visual sense, she doesn't have much sympathy for a painter who can't paint any more.
- Mark's lazy; all his talk about his muse departing. You don't wait around for inspiration. Sit down and get on with it.
- Maybe. It doesn't surprise me that Anna first has that shouting match with her best friend and then with Richard.
- Sarah lets her down, makes a decision without consulting her—

- You don't scream at your best friend when you have invited her to dinner, and others in the lounge hearing it. Anna wants to control everyone but she can't control herself.
- She's not perfect.
- I bet Richard bears the full brunt of her anger.
- He was late—
- Okay, but she managed without him and to shout at him, to me that was all about control. Control and her temper.
- That's you speaking now.
- As a reader, I can only speak as me. You told me that.
- Other people don't have such paranoid fears. You see control everywhere. If I ask you to tidy the newspaper, you complain that I'm controlling. If I ask you to put away the jumper you're not wearing, you complain about my control. I'm simply being practical. We both like a tidy house. If you don't put your things away, I have to do it.
- That's where Anna gets it from.
- And that's why you think she's not a nice character. Because you don't like me.
- Don't go away. I love you.

☙

- Good day?
- Okay. Yours?
- All right. What's Anna been up to?
- I've been working on Richard.
- And?
- There's something I want to check with you.
- I'm only a male reader.
- Exactly what I need: I'm trying to describe his first time.

9

- First time? First time having sex?
- The other.
- How am I supposed to know?
- Try.
- I can't promise.
- Also, what's his motivation? He has good sex at home.
- Maybe he wants something Anna isn't prepared to do.
- You forget that she's the more adventurous one. He's the vanilla man.
- Okay. Let's see: he's after a particular type of woman. Different from Anna. Fat. Huge breasts. Big bum.
- Is that what you like?
- Me? I'm talking about Richard.
- That's not him either.
- All right. He wants someone less assertive than Anna, someone who doesn't oppose him. He's running away from her controlling self.
- He hasn't got your paranoia.
- I can't see how Richard wouldn't mind.
- Mind what?
- Her control.
- He's never said anything.
- And whose responsibility is to make the character speak?
- It's not my fault. He doesn't say much.
- Make him. Make him complain.
- I need him like this.
- Okay: Richard loves being told what to do at home. He's deliriously happy with Anna organising everything.
- Don't be sarcastic.
- She'll be buying his clothes next.
- That's a good idea. Otherwise he might be wearing old

tweed jackets and corduroys. Anna can't stand that.
- Watch out, Richard. Stick to you your guns. Don't let her dress you.
- There're occasions when he feels hostile towards her, after an argument, and then he does take out his tweeds and corduroys.
- Good for him.
- It's childish. He knows it annoys her.
- That's her problem.
- What's the point of being in a relationship and deliberately doing things that annoy the other?
- You do.
- I don't.
- It annoys me when—
- This isn't about us. It's my novel we're talking about.
- Oh, really?
- Seriously, what would make a man who has good sex at home, an adventurous, attractive wife, seek a prostitute?
- Who knows?
- In fact, the stuff on sexuality I've been reading says there is no rational explanation.
- Why are you asking me, then?
- Something needs to trigger the first time. The narrative needs something, something that makes him contact a woman. You're a man. Think.
- I'm trying to.
- He could find a card. In a telephone box?
- Who goes to telephone boxes these days? It's the Internet now. That's where they advertise.
- Right.
- Perhaps he . . . comes across a site.

- Good day?
- Yes. Yours?
- Okay.
- Got it all worked out.
- Do you want me to read it?
- Not yet.
- What happens?
- The number to ring comes his way. By chance. He's on the train to Manchester, making notes, preparing a report for a meeting. He needs to stay overnight. He sees a paper someone's left behind, the *Manchester Evening News, Echo*, something like that. He notices the personal ads. One by a mature lady offering massage catches his attention. When he arrives in the hotel, his room's not ready and he has to wait. Sees the copy of the paper where someone has already looked through: the mature lady ad has been circled.
- Fate. Nothing to do with him.
- What do you mean?
- A chance event brings about an inevitable trajectory.
- I suppose so.
- Makes the reader think that Richard has to do it.
- Yes. Seeing the ad again puts a smile on his face but he still doesn't think about pursuing it. Later, in the room, he takes his papers out of the bag and the newspaper falls out: he accidentally brought it with him. He makes a bee line for the personals.
- He takes over from fate.
- He dials the number. On the spur of the moment, with no thought for the consequences.

- Out of curiosity. One often wonders what it's like to ring a number like that.
- Really?
- Or he could be doing it for a dare.
- Is that how you see it?
- Yes.
- Unprepared when she asks for his name, he gives the name of his boss.
- That's been done. There's a comic novel, where a guy does that and they tell him that they already have five people with that name.
- Anyway, they fix the arrangements. As he rings off, he's nervous, wants to cry off, decides to pay her at the door and say he's changed his mind. He goes downstairs and gets cash from the hole in the wall.
- Good thinking. I' sure it's cash only.
- She arrives. He's shocked: mature means she's in her sixties.
- Mustn't be ageist.
- Well, he's hardly being ageist. But would you expect a sixty plus woman to come when you ring a prostitute?
- How should I know? Some might like it.
- She has grotesque make up. He feels sorry for her. Pays her. They have a whisky. She chats a lot. Fat flabby arms spilling over the sides of the easy chair. She says that other rooms in the hotel are bigger than his. He feels uncomfortable with that.
- Naïve. He couldn't think she would be a virgin.
- I like his naiveté. Next, he decides he might just as well get something since he has paid. He asks her to suck him. She doesn't do oral. Massage, she says sternly. He settles for that, gets an erection. She is about to put a condom

on him but he ejaculates before she can open the packet.
- Oh, Richard. You could do better than that.
- What do you mean?
- A terrible let down.
- What can you expect when you pay a woman?
- Great service.
- You're not saying that.
- Sorry.
- Ultimately, it has to be a disappointing experience.
- Why?
- Necessary in narrative terms so he'll want another one to put this bad experience to rest. Only one, he'll think. But that idea comes later, once he's back. On the train, he thinks he's a lucky man: a successful career, an attractive wife, lovely children. He'd never do anything as stupid. The train is weaving past rolling hills with sheep grazing -
- Pastoral beauty after the ugliness of the previous night.
- Perhaps.
- It's not enough—
- ?
- Enough motivation. There must be something in him. That ad has to fall on fertile ground to germinate. He has to have a predisposition, be in the mood, the right frame of mind. He needs to be sexualised.
- ?
- Something needs to make him want to take action—
- He dials without thinking of anything.
- He may not be aware of it, but something's likely to have created that fertile ground; the newspaper is only the trigger.
- But what would you suggest?

- You're the author.
- You're a man. Put yourself in his situation.
- I'm not Richard.
- Think of something that happens to a man in everyday life. To sexualise him.
- Hmm. How about: a seriously crowded train, a woman pushes herself into him.
- And? People are always crushed together on trains.
- He's convinced she's doing it deliberately, masturbating. That turns him on.
- Your fantasy?
- We're talking about Richard.
- And then?
- Who's writing this novel?
- You're the male advisor.
- Okay. Squashed, Richard can't see her face; that's exciting.
- Your fantasy.
- You want my input or not?
- Sorry.
- He wonders what she looks like.
- Would he get an erection? Tell me, male reader.
- Quite likely. The train stops, people get off, he looks at them, wonders who she is.
- Admires her audacity. Remember, Richard likes strong women, women who take the initiative. Like Anna.
- Had a man behaved like that woman, a female passenger would have made a fuss. Called him a rapist, pervert.
- And so she should. But he isn't thinking of political correctness.
- He could feel offended. He should.
- Right, but he doesn't.

- If the author says so . . . What next?
- He goes home. He's looking forward to making love to Anna but—
- She isn't interested.
- Not quite. She's preoccupied with some problem at work, in her gallery, something that appears trivial to him, but she's a perfectionist and—
- More likely she's insensitive to his needs.
- You could say the same about him.
- Only if he insists on having sex. I can't imagine Richard doing that. Wouldn't the author agree?
- I suppose so.
- The way you've created Anna, she would be so obsessed with her problem and it wouldn't cross her mind to ask about his day. She wouldn't pay him any attention. He would be there only for her to unburden her worries.
- That's okay. That's what partners are for.
- That's what Richard's for.
- I disagree. This time she needs him. Next time, it may be the other way round.
- I bet she won't be there for him. You never seem to be there for me.
- This isn't about us.
- No?

❧

- How are you?
- Fine.
- Look, I'm sorry. I was tense yesterday . . . I'm sorry . . . I shouldn't have accused you of writing about us. I don't

know why I . . . well, I don't really, well, just sometimes, I feel for him. I know I shouldn't. He has nothing to do with me. I'm sorry, sorry about my tone.

- Okay. I didn't mind.
- You walked away.
- Yes. I don't know why. Sorry.
- I'm interested in what you write.
- You've never been touchy about characters before.
- I'm not touchy about him. I've been tired recently. That's why I overreacted.
- Can I help?
- It's fine. Tell me about those two.
- What do you want to know?
- What happens after that train journey? Richard's at home, sexualised, but she's worried about work. Presumably, they have dinner together.
- How about this: he tries to touch her hand but she's prickly. After dinner, she disappears to her study, he ends up in the bathroom, masturbating. Over the next few days he thinks about the woman, looks for her on the train. That same sensation, that sexual frisson comes back each time he gets on. He notices women sitting with their legs apart, women leaning forward, women wearing low cut tops.
- The ground's prepared.
- On the day of the train journey, I can see him walking home and imagining Anna waiting for him. You know Richard is old-fashioned, a bit like his parents who expected Anna to stay at home and look after the kids. He sees her in high heels and a fifties gathered skirt, all made up, standing in an immaculate kitchen, a fifties American ad. He knows the image is absurd and nothing to do with

17

their household. Not only is she in jeans and a jumper, as she often is, but she's not waiting for him. She's unloading the dishwasher and her thoughts are elsewhere.

- Why the fifties image?
- It says something about his hidden desire for a compliant Anna, an Anna like his mother, and his desire for the domesticity of his childhood. I think it says something about his difficulty reconciling his hidden, or not so hidden, desire with what Anna is. So he sees a woman with her hair done up, ondulated, or whatever they used to call it, standing in a kitchen that has no trace of use.
- Sometimes it seems to me that you novelists could keep a whole conference of psychiatrists busy for weeks on end.
- Now I have to decide how he uses the internet to get his women.
- Punternet.
- As in punter and net?
- Yes.
- One or two words?
- One. The net for punters.
- Where did you get that from?
- I can't remember.
- Mmm.
- I must've read about it somewhere.

⁂

- Sarah says I need another character.
- Why?
- She feels it's a bit claustrophobic.
- Claustrophobic? It's a novel about a relationship.

Relationships are claustrophobic.
- Do you think our marriage is claustrophobic?
- No.
- Why not?
- What do you mean: why not?
- You said relationships are claustrophobic. Why not ours?
- Bad relationships are claustrophobic. Where there is tension and—
- There is tension with us.
- Sometimes. That's normal.
- Tension and?
- Tension and what?
- You were saying tension and something else.
- I can't remember.

❧

- Had a long chat with Ursula this afternoon.
- Still struggling with the same poems. Bertran de Born has really taken over her life. She has no time for anyone else.
- No boyfriend?
- I don't know. She didn't mention anyone.
- You didn't ask?
- Never crossed my mind.
- Wouldn't you like her to have someone?
- She has friends.
- I mean, someone special.
- She has Bertran de Born.
- I mean someone real.
- He's real enough for her.
- You know what I mean. A real boyfriend.

- Why do you assume it's got to be a boyfriend?
- Oh, I forgot: everyone's bisexual.
- Good that you agree.
- You know I don't.
- Did I miss the sarcasm?
- You're the only person I know who says everyone's bisexual.
- That's unlikely. Most of our friends think the same.
- I doubt it but I bet Anna does.
- Come to think of it, yes, she does.
- How did I guess? What a coincidence.
- I don't like your tone.
- Sorry.
- Okay.
- Ursula, darling Ursula. So, it sounds like she's all right.
- Yes.
- Wouldn't you like her to have a relationship?
- It's up to her.
- Of course it's up to her. But I was asking what you would like.
- She's happy as she is, doing what she loves. That's good enough for me.
- I suppose so. I'm with Emma on that.
- You mean, what use is Provençal poetry to anyone?
- Exactly.
- I think you're wrong to talk of 'use'. De Born's lyrics are beautiful.
- Too remote from our experience.
- I disagree. Anyway, how many people really care or, to use your language, how many people find useful your research on women in politics or Emma's PhD on immigration? A minority. Probably not many more, not significantly more

than those who read Bertran de Born. And as for pleasure, it's all with Bertran de Born, none with your work.

- Not quite. At least we are about now, about changing our world. But an obscure mediaeval troubadour—
- Bertran de Born gives me pleasure. He gives pleasure to Ursula. That's two people. For me, even if we were the only ones, that would be enough. After all, how many people get pleasure from reading my novels?
- That's your choice. You could write more popular stuff.
- Popular stuff? Chick lit?
- It sells.
- And what kind of pleasure do readers get from reading even those so called literary novels? Voyeuristic.
- Innocuous. No harm in that.
- It's like wanting to know what happens behind the walls of your neighbours, peering in, prying.
- Stories can be educational. They give insight into the human condition.
- I don't want my novels to be manuals on how to behave, how to live. A novel is not a conduct book.
- Used to be. Who are you writing for?
- An intelligent, active reader, someone who is prepared to make an effort.
- No harm in being entertaining. Besides, your novel could contribute to the debate on prostitution.
- That's a politics academic speaking.
- Pleased to hear there's more to me than a male reader.
- I want my novel to transcend the story and the issue. I want more than that.
- That's quite a lot already. What else would you want it to be?

- Art.
- Meaning what?
- Unpredictable. New. Stylistically challenging. Like nothing before. Make readers see the world in a new way.
- Nothing new under the sun.
- Cliché.
- But true. Like most clichés.
- No point writing if you don't aim to produce something new.
- Of course there is: entertain your readers, help them cope with life, show them how to face adversity.
- I'm not a social worker, or an entertainer, or even a life-coach for that matter.
- So, why do you want to write about what happens to a couple when the woman discovers that the man had been seeing prostitutes for a good part of their marriage?
- I feel strongly about the issue.
- That should help your writing.
- Not sure about that.
- Isn't passion good? Strong views can be motivating.
- It could also hinder. But I was talking of something else.
- Which was?
- Particular topics invite particular treatment.
- You mean, if you were writing about waiting for some Godot, or about your mother omitting to kiss you good night and agonizing about that until you and your readers lose the will to live . . . you could experiment but not with this.
- Yes, I worry that my story doesn't lend itself to experimental treatment.
- You may be right.

- But I don't want to accept it. I wonder whether Anna's search for answers is like waiting for Godot? Or perhaps Marcel's agony brought on by the failure of his mother to kiss him good night is comparable to what she goes through. Or even what Richard suffers.
- I can't answer that. Not my *métier*. What else did you say to Ursula?
- I told her about Richard and Anna.
- And?
- Ursula thinks that if anything like that had happened to us, she would disown you. She'd never want to be under the same roof with you.
- Unforgiving Ursula.
- She said what Richard does is not so much to do with betraying Anna, but betraying all women. It's the buying aspect, the treatment of women as a commodity, that's what she wouldn't be able to take.
- Ursula's being pompous.
- My good feminist daughter.
- In a family, people have to help each other. Not walk out. I'm sure Emma would take a different view.
- Possibly. Ursula wondered whether I should make his job connected to something with women.
- ?
- Promoting women's rights.
- As long as he's not known for his research into women in the Labour Party.
- Why haven't I thought of it?
- Don't you dare!
- Oh, I know: an academic specialising in . . . suffragettes.
- No, too close.

- You're paranoid.

※

- Richard could be sacked from work.
- Why? Seeing prostitutes isn't a crime.
- No, but using his work computer to access porn and to contact the women is a sackable offence.
- Technically, yes. He shouldn't be so unlucky.
- He's done horrible things.
- Using prostitutes isn't illegal.
- It should be.
- That's a different matter. By the way, have you decided what he does?
- Something professional. Something clever. He's successful. But he also has very low self-esteem.
- Why?
- Men who regularly use prostitutes often suffer from low self-esteem, even when they're professionally very successful.
- Punters come from all walks of life, don't they?
- Yes. But it's men like Richard who interest me. Why is it that they resort to prostitutes? Therapists claim that most men don't go for sex. And if it isn't sex, then it rankles even more. Because you can't find the answer. Some research suggests there's something in their past, in their upbringing, in the way their mother treated them that creates a predisposition.
- Perhaps. A prostitute is easier than an affair. No baggage. Less threatening to a relationship.
- More horrible for the man's partner. With an affair, at least

you can think your husband fell in love with someone; it happened. With a prostitute, it's the deliberate setting out to deceive.

- But it's simple. No emotional interference in the marriage. No threat. If I had to seek something outside our relationship, I'd imagine paying would be less threatening to us. A real woman—
- A real woman? Prostitutes aren't real women?
- You know what I mean.
- I don't expect you to use such language. Not the man who's made a career out of arguing for women's political representation.
- Okay. Sorry, it was just shorthand.
- Sometimes shorthand reveals our prejudices.
- What I'm saying is that seeing a prostitute is less likely to undermine one's relationship than having an affair, an emotional attachment that can get out of hand—
- Things can get out of hand with prostitutes.
- With Richard, having prostitutes means the affection he has for Anna doesn't need to be shared—
- A spurious argument. As if one had a limited pot of affection.
- But If I had to seek something outside—
- What is this 'if I had to'?
- I don't know. This is hypothetical. But if so, would you prefer I had an affair or went to a prostitute?
- That's not a choice. Hang on. Are you trying to tell me something?
- No!
- Do I need to point out to you that only a male can argue like you do—

- I am male—
- I mean, a sexist male, a politically unaware male—
- Look, it's obvious. Having an affair, you may fall in love, or your fellow affairist—
- Affairist?
- The person you're having an affair with.
- No such word.
- I just made it up. You always do.
- I'm a writer.
- All right. You have the prerogative to make up words. What I'm saying is your lover, she can fall in love with you, and you with her, and that can cause complications, make her demanding, etc. Nothing like that with a prostitute.
- Everything you're saying only works provided the secret life remains secret. Besides, you're not taking into consideration the political, ideological wrong.
- ?
- Don't tell me you don't understand: buying women is morally wrong.

❧

- Good day?
- Yes. Yours?
- Fine, thank you.
- What great things happened today?
- Figures.
- ?
- Frightening figures. Depressing figures.
- ?
- Did you know that one in nine British men has paid for

sex?
- Really?
- Many more than I thought. Gone up recently. No shame attached to it any more. Men freely admit to it. All walks of life, all races, all ages.
- Mmm.
- As for women, there are around 100,000 who sell sex.
- Supply and demand.
- It's not a simple question of the market, or of the statistics, such as a sex worker for every 300 men.
- No?
- It's a question of ruined lives on both sides.
- Some pleasure as well.
- You can't say that.
- What about the men who are disfigured, severely disabled and can't find anyone? Isn't it better for them to pay—
- No, it isn't.
- What can they do?
- What about the poor women? What we want is a world where disabled people are seen as valid sexual partners.
- A tall order.
- Achievable.
- I still think prostitutes are selling a service.
- What those men are buying is not a service; it's mastery of the woman's body.
- Some women freely choose to do it—
- Freely choose - no such thing. Forced by pimps or circumstances.
- Some women are forced by circumstances to become cleaners.
- That's a job.

- Often on very low pay.
- Another issue. You can't compare it to being forced into prostitution, an intrusion into your body, into your most intimate self.
- I was only thinking aloud.
- Aloud and without any sense.
- Some prostitutes are on record saying they regard it as a job. They have ways of switching off.
- That's all right, then? What does it do for their sense of identity?
- They don't worry about it. In any case, they're not the only ones who have to resort to switching off at work. Think of those on assembly lines, or millions of people, the majority even, doing unpleasant dull jobs—
- There's no comparison. No matter how much she chooses and consents to paid sex, a prostitute is raped each time.
- That's going too far.
- How much do you know about how a woman feels letting a stranger do what he likes to her body? A sex worker isn't the same as a hairdresser.
- No. Blow dries are different from blow jobs.
- Don't be facetious.
- What's to be done? Legalisation? Have it in the open, help the women, allow them to report violence.
- No, it hasn't worked in Holland. The only thing is to help the women get out and criminalise the men. As in Sweden.
- Your novel might make a contribution to the debate. You have to write it. Experimental or not. You'll find a way.
- One thing I'm sure of: there should be no price on a woman's body.

- A powerful sentence. One of your characters should say that.

- A good day?
- Yes. You?
- Okay. Who was it?
- Richard.
- What happened?
- I know what he does.
- Yes?
- He's an academic.
- No! Don't tell me he's in politics, has a PhD and does research on women in the Labour Party.
- Don't be silly. Richard is a suffragette historian.
- That's too close. I told you I don't like it. Why do you have to take everything from our lives?
- Only a few details.
- What will people think?
- I couldn't make him a . . . I don't know . . . a . . . physicist. There would be no irony. A chap in a lab, working on gravity, or whatever they do, buying sex. Lacks that extra dimension. But a man who has made his career out of promoting women's rights, going on about the importance of women's right to vote and then that same chap goes out and buys women as if they were commodities. Much richer.
- People are bound to make the connection.
- ?
- With me.
- You?

- Yes, me. Don't look so surprised.
- You aren't Richard. This is fiction. Everyone knows that.
- Most people assume a novel is based on the writer's own experience.
- I can't help it if uneducated readers think everything is autobiographical.
- You can. You don't have to make him like me.
- You aren't him.
- ?
- Are you?
- ?
- No point raising your eyebrows. This man has been seeing prostitutes for eight years and he—
- You could make him do some other job, such as . . .
- What?
- Oh, I don't know. There are millions of jobs.
- Okay, give me one. Got to be professional.
- He's a doctor.
- No good.
- A gynaecologist. Aha, that's good. Helping women.
- No.
- A plastic surgeon. Helping women get the breasts they want.
- Dubious.
- How many breast surgeons do we know?
- It's the image I don't like. It stands for something un-comfortable. In any case, Richard being a breast surgeon wouldn't work.
- Please, think of something else. Make him . . . I don't know.
- Suffragette historian is perfect. I've got it all sorted out.
- What do you mean?

- The work side. The way he's discovered. The meetings with his head of department.
- I hope he's not called Bob.
- He is, but I can change that if you are worried your Bob might not like it—
- Might not like it! Haven't you got any imagination? What about one of those baby name books? Look it up there.
- I will. This is work in progress.
- My colleagues read your books.
- I'm glad to hear it.
- No Bob under any circumstances.
- Okay. I'll come up with something else. But it's a pity. A good name for the character I have in mind. The head who's a few years older than Richard, a good administrator but without much of an academic record. Richard's CV, of course, is impeccable. I see this Bob as being embarrassed about the whole situation, reluctant to use the word prostitute, ashamed to say it aloud. He fumbles with papers, he speaks in a roundabout way. Richard finds him irritating, particularly his habit of not coming straight to the point on any issue.
- Don't you understand how embarrassing this could be for me?
- This is a novel. Anyway, this head keeps saying those . . . those . . . and then he pauses, he doesn't dare use the word prostitutes; eventually he says, those, those girls. Richard doesn't understand what he means and then Bob comes up with those working girls. Richard is inflamed. Girls. At least call them women, he says. And you are preaching to me, he says, you with your sexist talk. Bob's an old fool.
- Like mine. Please, no Bob.

- Okay. As an old fool, he doesn't understand what all the fuss is all about. He feels that men have always been paying for sex. He has to quote another colleague, Myra, a woman who, as he says, has been going on about the politics of Richard's actions. When he uses the word politics, Richard jumps up. Politics has nothing to do with this, he says. It's between Anna and me. Does she know, Bob asks—
- Not Bob.
- Don't worry. This is just a working name.
- As long as it doesn't stick.
- It won't.
- But it's a good question.
- Which question?
- Does Anna know?
- Not as yet. He's still thinking it can be hushed up and he would get away without having to speak to Anna.
- A bit of a long shot.
- I suppose so but Richard's a desperate man at this point. He can't think clearly. He can only hope. So Richard tells Bob—
- There's no Bob.
- Right: Richard tells the man formerly known as Bob—
- Please, take it seriously. I've given in on so many other details, but not on this.
- Fine, so Richard says that's none of his business, I mean none of the business of . . . his head of department, or anyone else, whether Anna knows or not. Then he adds: if you want to know, I paid those women what they asked for. They were lucky to have me rather than the Yorkshire Ripper.
- Why would he say that?

- In anger.
- Too cocky in the circumstances.
- In bad taste too. He shouldn't have said it; no doubt about that. He immediately regrets it.
- Does his boss comment?
- He says: 'Not for me to say.' Idiot.
- How's Richard discovered?
- A group of sociology students, post-graduates, go around and take photos of men entering massage parlours and houses where sex workers operate. Their campaign is to shame the men, abolish prostitution.
- Revolutionary bra burners.
- They want to make prostitution illegal. They catch him entering a house of a woman in Chiswick. They take a snap of him coming out just over an hour later.
- Did you make that up or are there such groups?
- I haven't come across one but if they don't exist, they should. Perhaps a woman's group might get the idea from the novel.
- Direct intervention. The novel changing reality.
- Why not?
- It's only that you always say you don't like that kind of fiction.
- It's not that I don't like it. What I mean is that, to my mind, changing the world isn't the novel's primary function. That's not why I write.
- Still, it could be a powerful side effect. What do they do with the pictures?
- Don't know. Maybe they are building an archive for some action later, some campaigning. Maybe they put it up on social media. Or, they could blackmail the men and build

up a fund to help sex workers who want to get out.

- Blackmail is a crime.
- Okay. Just a thought. An amusing one: men financing the destruction of prostitution.
- They recognise Richard as they are looking at the photos.
- Exactly. They go to see the VC and threaten demos unless he's sacked. Fearing bad publicity, the university has to act but at the same time they can't sack him for seeing a prostitute. Bob—
- No Bob, please. There's no Bob in this novel.
- Sorry, he arranges a sabbatical. Richard refuses to take it despite the fact that normally he would have welcomed a year off teaching. Eventually, they find out something else – not sure as yet what. He's forced to resign.
- Wow. What now?
- What would you advise?
- I don't know: he really is in the shit.
- In shit of his own making.

※

- Good day?
- So so.
- Oh. What about you?
- Not much to say. What has Richard done today?
- Nothing.
- Nothing?
- I worked on Tanya.
- Tanya?
- Yes, the young prostitute who comes to a conscious-ness-raising group Anna used to run with Sara why they

were postgraduates.

- Oh, yes. Why?
- Why what? Why have I worked on her?
- No, why does she come to the group?
- Anna and Sarah have been distributing leaflets about their group in the city centre. They would like to expand and bring in more members from outside the university.
- Middle class guilt?
- That's you again. I don't believe in it. Those two don't suffer from it, either. No, they are interested in campaigning on women's issues. They don't just want to read academic articles. They don't want to discuss feminism without putting it into practice.
- Commendable, if a trifle patronizing.
- They want to campaign to help sex workers, against domestic violence, for equal pay and so on.
- And, this young prostitute, how old is she?
- Tanya's nineteen.
- She comes to the group and then what?
- She's the only one who comes as a result of the leaflets. And she doesn't tell them what she does. They assume she's a student.
- Typical. But why does she come? What's in it for her?
- She hopes to get something out of it for herself. She lives with a boyfriend who pimps her and is violent.
- I think you told me that already. A bit of a cliché?
- Maybe. Very common though, much too common to leave it out of a story like this one.
- I see.
- I hope she's not all cliché. I don't think she's your tart with a golden heart. She's rough.

- I suppose most of them are. They don't have a choice.
- Right. But she's rough when it comes to her child too. She's not sentimental.
- Oh, yes. You did say she had a child.
- A two-year-old girl who cries a lot and that irritates the boyfriend. So he hits Tanya for not being able to control the child. But then he hits her for everything. If she doesn't bring in enough money, or simply if he's angry, drunk or anything else. When Tanya gets the leaflet, she has the idea that talking to other women might help. She wants to ask them what to do.
- What about the women she works with?
- They tell her to leave him.
- Good advice.
- She doesn't see it like that.
- So, what does she do?
- At first, she goes to a meeting in town but it's been cancelled, or rather, moved to a different venue. When she checks where it is and realises it's on campus, she is put off. That's not a word she knows. It makes her think of camp sites.
- Is that plausible?
- Why not? I remember telling a woman on a bus once, in my student days, that I lived on campus and she thought that I lived in a caravan or in a tent.
- Okay. I wouldn't know.
- When Tanya finds out that it's the university, she's terrified. She was trouble at school. Teachers hated her. She is not going 'back to school'. But a week or so later she's badly beaten and she remembers the leaflet said the group was for women only and for women who want to help each

36

other. She goes there to meet other women and see what she can get from them.

- Why doesn't she leave him?
- She doesn't dare. He threatens to come after her. Besides, he persuades her that the flat was given to both of them and if she leaves, she won't get another one from the council and how would she survive with a child on the street?
- Do the women help her?
- We see her walking across the campus square in front of the library, picking her way and cursing her high heels. She doesn't have any other shoes. All her shoes are work shoes. Understandably, she's nervous. She has spent a long time deciding what to wear. She's conscious of her appearance; she looks different from everyone around her.
- Poor Tanya.
- When she arrives, most of the women are helpful and welcome her, but there is one who Tanya feels she ought to watch.
- Does she stay?
- Yes, but she feels completely out of it. They are reading an article by Gayatry Chakravorty Spivak.
- Good old Gayatry. I remember you reading that stuff when we first met.
- Do you? Thirty odd years ago?
- Yes. You used to give me passionate accounts of each piece. Didn't you even meet her once at a conference?
- Yes, I did. I remember being struck by her whole demean-our and appearance: a sari and a short, punkish haircut. Haven't thought about her for ages but I believe she's still active. Still read by students.
- Oh yes. Not by anyone else, I'd think.

- That's unfortunate because she is one of the few academics who has written and cared about ordinary women, one of those whose feminism wasn't confined to academia. That's why it's appropriate she's on the agenda when Tanya arrives.
- Much beyond her, I'd think. And I wouldn't imagine many of your readers would be interested either.
- I don't know. But Tanya certainly can't make any sense out of what's going on, either with the group or with the article. At the same time, she dares not leave—
- Do you really think so? A street walker? She'd be tough. Wouldn't she be able to look after herself?
- I'd think that her toughness works in her milieu. Not among postgrads. With them, she's tongue-tied, almost shy. A fish out of water.
- I see.
- They are sitting round a large table with coffee, tea and cakes in the middle. Even the cake is strange: carrot, not something she would have ever heard of. She spills coffee over the photocopy they give her and feels even more rotten: she remembers how clumsy she was at school. Eventually, the meeting ends as a seminar group knocks on the door; the women have overrun.
- I remember meeting you after those groups. You were always late.
- I'm never late.
- You were.
- I don't think so. We had a flexible arrangement. That's why we tended to meet in the journals room of the library so that the other could read while waiting.
- I never made you wait.

- You never gave me time to read the journals.
- Sorry. I thought you would have appreciated my eagerness to be with you.
- I did.
- And with this group, you have it all worked out? I mean, what will happen later?
- Not quite. I was thinking of an occasion where we had a woman coming to a session and it was so obvious that she didn't belong. I'm not sure whether it was a question of class. But perhaps it was something else. Perhaps she was foreign; you could just tell from her body language that she felt uncomfortable. I was thinking of her while writing about Tanya.
- Using real life again—
- In this case, it's transformed experience: the awkwardness of a foreigner becomes the awkwardness of a prostitute.
- Tanya never comes back, I assume.
- She rushes out as soon as the chance presents itself but Anna and Sarah catch up with her.
- Arh, those two. They won't let her go.
- Right. She can't believe how they manage to catch up with her but then, unlike them, she doesn't know shortcuts through the building's corridors and she is slow picking her way in her high heels. I imagine her being self-conscious as her shoes click on the hard floor – in fact, that's the thing I remember about that woman, that foreign woman. It was all clickety-click and she seemed to be self-conscious of her every step and the noise it made.
- So, those two catch up with her.
- Yes, and they go on about how pleased they are that she came to the group.

- Two busy-bodies. They can't be sincere.
- I think they are but Tanya doesn't believe them. Anyway, she has decided she will never come back but she doesn't tell them that. When they ask her which department she's in, she says she would like to be a teacher – the words surprise her; she doesn't know where they come from; she hated her teachers. The women think Tanya's in education. Sarah even says something like oh, then you must know Jonathan, my flat mate, the young lecturer, and Tanya nods. They invite her to come with them to a Bergman film on Saturday night—
- Bergman? For a prostitute? That would sort her out.
- Don't be facetious. They don't know she isn't a student.
- Most students wouldn't watch Bergman.
- Well, Anna and Sarah do.
- Because you do.
- Okay. Tanya doesn't go to see Bergman.
- Surprise, surprise.
- She tells them that she has something on. Even if she wanted to go with them, Saturday night is her busiest night. The women agree it's too short notice and promise to tell her about the next meeting well in advance. Tanya breathes a sigh of relief as they part.
- I think I would too.
- I thought you liked Bergman.
- Some of it. But it's those two. Imposing busy-bodies.
- They're well meaning.
- They may be but they have no idea what life's like for her.
- True.
- And if they did, they wouldn't know what to do, how to help her.

- Maybe. But you can't deny they are friendly.
- Overbearing more like it.
- I suppose that's what it might feel like to Tanya. Anyway, she has to rush home because her neighbour, Mrs Bhatta, who's been looking after her daughter, the two year old Lilla, has to leave for her afternoon shift at Cadbury's.
- Right. They're in Birmingham. At least it's not Bristol.
- Don't worry; I'm not pinching from our student days.
- Which reminds me, I was going to ask you: how did Anna and Richard meet? Hope it wasn't at a Labour Party evening and then—
- No, they met at an outing in a restaurant, some birthday or other of a mutual friend and the second time when they talked properly and when, you could say, the relationship started was as they ran into each other outside the university library.
- No!
- Look, we can't be the only couple who had a chat outside the library and started going out after that.
- You could think of so many other occasions, so many other venues.
- But this is just as good. It doesn't reveal anything about us. I need the library; I don't want them to meet in a pub.
- You mean they need to give the impression of being intellectual.
- They are intellectual.
- Intellectual people go to pubs.
- I don't.
- Well, others do.
- Anna and Richard don't. Meeting outside the library shouldn't bother you. It should not be as important as

Bob to you.
- What's he called now?
- Still thinking.
- Carry on thinking.
- It's difficult. Bob suits him perfectly. You know how important names are to novelists. They are part of the overall characterization. Bob communicates so perfectly his fumbling, clumsy self.
- Look, you can have the library conversation, you can even have them in Bristol, but you can't have Bob.
- Don't worry.

❧

- Has Bob been rechristened?
- Rechristened?
- Well, my Bob was brought up Catholic. Once a Catholic . . .
- That's brilliant. Fits in perfectly.
- What?
- Bob's Catholicism and his reluctance to mention the word prostitute, his oppressive sexuality. Bob's not malicious, he has the best of intentions, he wants to help Richard, Richard's his most valuable member of staff and he can't afford to lose him. But secretly he enjoys talking about sex and normally he would feel guilty but that is assuaged by the situation: now it's his duty to talk about sex. Whenever the two of them meet - at first Richard insists that they meet on campus, in Bob's—
- Look, that's all well and good. But please put my mind at rest and give him another name.
- Bob's only his working name. I'll change it later.

- And the RAE and Richard's academic record? The similar-
  ity to my position in the department is, of course, 'entirely
  coincidental'.
- Of course. Every department has someone who is much
  better at research than the rest. You're only one of many
  people in that position. Richard has to have an enviable
  academic record – important part of the story.
- Even that I can accept but Bob, no. He has to be renamed.

⚜

- Good day?
- Not bad. Yours?
- Same as usual.
- Good.
- Did you know there are middle-class women who operate
  from their homes?
- Prostitutes?
- Yes. That's why I made Richard visit one in Chiswick.
- A bit too close.
- You think we might meet her.
- I can see you walking in the area and choosing a house
  for the chapter.
- No, I didn't do that. She's fictional, based on punters'
  accounts. Don't worry.
- I'm surprised why you chose an area near to us.
- No particular reason. All I needed was a middle class street
  with good property prices. She lives in a big house, alone,
  or that's what Richard assumes when he notices one tooth-
  brush and one dressing gown in the bathroom.
- There could be another bathroom, or two.

- Of course. She has a posh accent and he wonders whether she's a widow or a divorcee, fallen on hard times. When he arrives, he finds the situation disconcerting—
- Why? I'd have thought he's well used to—
- A different type of woman. Most of his are poor, working class, or oriental, immigrants.
- A break from his usual routine.
- Exactly. He has a way of speaking to those women but he can't use that with this one. Most of the others come to him in hotel rooms or he goes to their flats, basement places with horrible wallpaper and stained carpets and after he has given them the money - cash, always cash, of course which, by the way, he tends to hand over in an envelope—
- Is this usual?
- I don't think so. I can't picture a punter putting cash in an envelope or worrying about it.
- You seem to have a clichéd image in mind.
- Do I?
- Didn't you say punters come from all walks of life? If I were to—
- You would use an envelope?
- Yes, I would. Looks more decent, dignified.
- I see. In Richard's case that's only part of the reason.
- ?
- It's not only out of respect for the women but he also does it for himself—
- Meaning?
- He prefers not to have to look at the money. That way he can pretend that he's having an affair.
- Poor sod.
- Apparently, that's quite common, I mean, men trying to

forget that money has changed hands. They often write how the woman liked them.

- I see.
- Anyway, once he hands over the cash – always the first thing, always at the beginning – he can get on with the small talk. Not with this Chiswick woman. She places the envelope on the mantelpiece and he is conscious of it being there, staring at him.
- Come on Richard, make an effort.
- Are you cheering for him?
- I feel sorry for him being so, so . . . pathetic.
- Dishonest and stupid, more likely.
- Stupid, yes.
- The woman calls herself Adele and discloses her real name as he's to leave. I only give it to the gentlemen I can trust, she says. Next time, ask for Jennifer, Jen.
- Is there going to be next time?
- Richard doesn't go twice to the same woman.
- Why?
- It's never satisfactory. He thinks with someone else he might have that fulfilment, the ultimate experience.
- Poor chap.
- Idiot. Now, Adele's different from his other women. Her house is in a tree-lined street and although not in good nick, it's a large Georgian building on three floors with a basement, the kind of house Anna likes, he thinks.
- Would he be thinking of Anna at that point?
- He does.
- Wouldn't a man at that point try to forget about his wife?
- Not necessarily. It's compartmentalisation; the ability to separate the two lives. It doesn't mean that he forgets that

he's married to Anna when he goes to see a sex worker. But he makes himself think the two lives are separate; one doesn't impinge on the other. Anyway, he remembers that she's an architect manqué—

- What a surprise. Why should she be an architect manqué?
- A bit of characterisation.
- But why take it from you?
- I'm not the only person who wanted to be an architect: Obama, for one.
- There could be something else about the house that makes him think of Anna, if that's what you want. Flowers in the front garden. How about that?
- I don't see why this bothers you? Part of me is given to Anna, not part of you.
- More and more those two are like us.
- They aren't. I find the idea of architect manqué amusing. My private joke. It's rather like when Hitchcock walks through a scene.
- People who know us will recognise it as you and they'll assume the story is ours.
- People who know us will be able to see this is fiction.
- I doubt it. A question: does he tend to make arrangements with his women after disagreements with Anna?
- You mean so he could blame her later when it all comes out? It's possible he uses that to justify his action to himself.
- It would make sense: he feels low when they have an argument and he rings prostitutes to make himself feel better.
- Is that what you would do?
- I'm only making suggestions. Now, he's outside the house, thinking about Anna. Is he wondering whether to change

his mind?

- No, but secretly he's always hoping that the woman wouldn't be in or that something would happen at the last minute, a train crash, something that would prevent him from having to go through with it.
- He could cancel.
- More often than not, he does, but has to keep some to make the game appear credible to himself. The excitement is in the anticipation—
- And that excitement is mixed with fear.
- Exactly. Absolute terror at the prospect of meeting the women.
- Poor Richard.
- Despite the fear, he goes on making arrangements. No wonder it doesn't make sense to Anna. He's an intelligent man and yet he keeps putting himself through all this.
- I think he would be able to see it in someone else. It's harder to be aware of one's own madness. And since you haven't given him a close friend, there's no one to point it out to him.
- Are you saying that it's the author's fault?
- Possibly.
- Always blame the woman.
- That's one way of looking at it.
- As for compartmentalising, remember, he has a different identity when he visits the women. That helps too.
- I see.
- He's called Alan, Alan Roberts. That was the name he gave to the old woman in Manchester, the first one. You remember the name of the guy he was meeting, the head of history.

- The head of history?
- Yes, but if any of the women ask him about his work, he says he's a school teacher, maths or physics—
- Why?
- They always ask. Part of the small talk. And maths or physics, he reckons, is furthest from history.
- But the women wouldn't care what he does.
- They only ask to make conversation.
- What happens with the posh woman?
- Adele. Right, as I said, he finds her unnerving because the game is different. First the house, then her. After opening the door wearing a short, see-through negligée, she offers him wine. None of the others have done that.
- And there's the envelope on the mantelpiece.
- Yes, disconcerting.
- I can see this will be another disappointment.
- Quite right. So, Richard, or Alan, as he is now, and this woman sit in her lounge, sipping wine. She apologises for the untidiness. Again not the kind of thing any other woman has said. If only he could forget about the envelope, he could pretend he's with a friend, a lover. He says he likes her house. It looks lived in. He thinks of what Anna tends to say: lived in - just a stupid excuse for people to be messy, too lazy to tidy their stuff. She's always trying to turn their Edwardian house into a minimalist loft.
- All our friends will recognize you here.
- A little joke.
- It won't be so funny when they assume it's about us.
- You underestimate them. They know a novel is not real.
- Most people read because they take it for reality.
- I don't like most people.

- Don't I know it?
- Can we stop being personal? Let's get back to Richard. When he looks around the house, he is actually psyching himself. Don't you think?
- You mean building up his resentment against Anna—
- Exactly. That assuages any possible guilt, makes him feel better, justifies his session with the whore. His armchair is a couple of metres from hers and he would like to move closer, touch her, put his hand on her breasts but he doesn't dare, it doesn't seem appropriate with this kind of conversation.
- Is she the only middle-class one?
- For Richard? Yes, I think so.
- Wouldn't he have worked it all out in advance? Planned his moves, what to say.
- He didn't anticipate she would be so different.
- Do your homework next time, Richard.
- Don't encourage him.
- I don't think he listens to me; he's a fictional character, as you keep telling me.
- Yes, but it disturbs me when you're on his side; it makes me think that you approve of his—
- Does he get anywhere with Adele?
- They are still talking in the lounge when she mentions her garden and asks him if he wants to see it.
- They will do it outside?
- That's Richard's first thought.
- Obviously.
- But no, they don't; it's too cold. He's both polite and apprehensive. But he fantasises about sex in the shed; he can see cushions through the window and thinks how exciting

it would be to lie there. Have urgent sex. He feels his erection stirring.

- He's paid her. He should tell her what he wants.
- He doesn't dare; he feels she's too much in control. She makes him listen to a water feature.
- Poor old Richard.
- Don't say that.
- Sorry.
- Eventually, they go upstairs but she stops him and asks him to take off his shoes. She has a cream-coloured runner on the stairs.
- A man in socks. That should be sobering.
- What do you mean?
- Cuts you down to size when you take shoes off.
- I suppose so. Not only does he obey but he also apologizes, saying that he should have thought of it.
- She'll have him eating from her hand.
- In the bedroom, she gives him a towel and asks him to have a wash. He had a shower before leaving home but he doesn't argue.
- What a wimp!
- In the bathroom, he avoids his face in the large mirror behind the sink. He's afraid he might lose his nerve. You see that's where I imagined his sobering moment: washing his penis, his clean penis, in someone else's bathroom strikes him as absurd and for a split second he feels like walking out but he makes an effort to wash without thinking about the situation. The absurdity carries on: he feels silly pulling up his trousers when he's about to take them off a second later but it would be even more ridiculous to walk in with the trousers around his ankles.

- A Charlie Chaplin moment, shuffling along.
- Right.
- You can work out details without stealing from real life when you want to.
- It interests me what goes through the mind of an intelligent, articulate, happily married man at a moment like that—
- Is he happily married?
- Both of them think so.
- A big question mark.
- Yes, but if they both think so, then it must be—
- Is ours a happy marriage?
- What do you mean?
- Do you think we have a happy marriage?
- Do you?
- I asked first.
- I'm trying to talk about my novel but you always turn it into a discussion about us.
- Because it's about us.
- No it isn't.
- And then?
- They have sex.
- They do?
- Sort of. They have oral but then his mobile goes off. For a few seconds he doesn't realise it's his. He loses his erection. Despite her efforts, he can't get it back.
- You're using the phone like some *deus ex machina*.
- A useful device. He thinks he can't get his erection back because it bothers him that she's too much in charge. She keeps telling him what to do and ignores what he says he wants. His other whores do not behave like that.

- Poor Richard.
- Serves him right.
- Maybe therapy will sort him out. Maybe all this has to happen so that he emerges a better person.
- This isn't Richard's Bildungsroman.

❧

- Good day?
- Don't ask.
- Why?
- Done nothing.
- How come?
- I don't know.
- Have you run out of ideas?
- No. But I was scared.
- Scared of what?
- The usual thing.
- The usual thing?
- I've looked over what I've got so far and it's not right—
- The first draft. You can work on it later. I don't need to tell you that.
- It's different this time.
- Because it's about us.
- It's not about us.
- Then why?
- I don't know. It's always scary, always scary as if it were my first time. I read somewhere about a writer - a writer who has published thirty odd books - saying that when it comes to his work, he is permanently a virgin. I feel like that: it's always the first time, always scary, no matter how

many books you've done.
- What are you scared of?
- Failure.
- Failure?
- Yes, what I have in my head, the voice I hear, the words I see in my mind, the tone, it's never as good as when I put it on paper. It's always inferior. So sometimes you feel you want to keep it in your mind, preserve the idea for ever, rather than write it down. It's like Keats' Grecian Urn: as long as the love isn't realised, consummated, as long as the lovers are suspended in the act of trying to reach each other, they live with the anticipation of ideal love. Painted on a Grecian urn, they remain forever stuck in the moment, forever inhabiting a universe of desire and ideal, forever unable to realise their love, but also forever away from divorce and quarrels and betrayals and the rest of the ugly stuff. It's the same with writing. If you want the ideal, if you want perfect writing, you shouldn't write it down. It should stay in your head.
- But no one would be able to see it.
- Perhaps you could just talk about it. Go for long walks with your readers and tell them about the novel you're writing but in fact you're not writing it because if you were, the result would be a disappointment.
- Like that guy—
- Jack Toledano.

⚘

- How was your day?
- Not good.

- Why?
- I keep wondering whether I've taken a wrong turning.
- A wrong turning?
- In the story. Little decisions that a novelist makes to move the story along.
- And then one leads to another and that in turn . . . but if one of them doesn't feel right, the mistakes augment, the wrong turning snowballs and you end up in an impasse.
- Exactly. You speak like a novelist. Except for mixing your metaphors.
- Mixing metaphors? Oh, I see. You have me there. But this problem arises in any writing. All a matter of structure, of organising your argument, your story line. Can I help?
- No one can. I may have to retrace my steps—
- You mean, undo some of the narrative?
- Yes. Unknit it, like a jumper. Take a different turning at some point in the narrative and see if it works. The problem is to know where.
- Make Richard a nicer person.
- I thought you already liked him. You had problems with Anna.
- Both of them. You never see them being happy together. It makes you wonder whether the marriage was as good as they claim.
- It's difficult to have flashbacks, happy flashbacks, because the past is bound to be coloured by what happened. That's another thing that hurts Anna so much.
- What do you mean?
- Her memories of happy occasions, holidays and birthdays, all of that has to be revised. She looks at their photographs, at the smiling faces and she's angry that so much was going

on but she didn't know it. How could she be smiling, she asks herself, when Richard, looking so happy, his arms around her, had just booked such and such a woman. It's not only my present, and perhaps my future, but also my past, that have been taken from me, she says. She can try to influence her present and her future, but there's nothing she can do about her past. It's gone and it was horrible but she didn't even know it.

- It wasn't horrible at the time. She should remember it as it felt then.
- To her the memory is false. Has to be revised. She wonders how she could have been so stupid. She's hurt by the idea that she lived a life that wasn't what she thought it was. Was she too focused on the girls, on the gallery, did she neglect Richard? How else could she have missed what he was up to?
- That's sad and readers might have sympathy but if you want her to be liked, she can't go on rolling in the mud. She has to pick herself up and move forward.
- You're insensitive. Can't you see how hurt she is?
- Let her lick her wounds and get on with life. Smell the roses.
- She could do that if she left him. Then it would be mainly a question of sorting herself out. But if she stays, she can't repair the marriage on her own.
- She can start by playing her part.
- She doesn't think Richard's helping.
- ?
- She needs him to show her how much he cares for her. That is, if he does. And I'm not sure he does. Anna doubts it too. She's more vulnerable and needs more attention

than before. He doesn't seem to understand.

- Self-centred as always. She wants him to pay the price for what he has done.
- How is being attentive to your wife paying a price? It should be a joy. A privilege.
- He needs attention too. It's obvious he's screwed up.
- He has his therapist.
- It's not the same. Anna always sees everything in terms of herself.
- That's what you think of me, don't you?
- I was talking about her. In any case, she could have therapy if she wanted to.
- Rachel wasn't any help.
- Typical of Anna's impetuosity to walk out on her therapist.
- Why do you say she's impetuous?
- Well, you are.
- So? Anna's not me.
- More or less she is.
- Are you Richard?
- You're building him out of me.
- Rubbish. Do you have a secret life?
- Don't be ridiculous. When would I have the time?
- That's exactly what Richard says.
- Does he?
- Once he's late and claims he was at a meeting in the department. Anna says she tried to contact him but the secretary said he had already left. Richard claims the secretary got it wrong. Anna believes him – she shouldn't, as we know – but half-jokingly she adds, perhaps you were with some woman you are keeping secret from me. That's when he comes up with that sentence.

- Is Anna being serious?
- No, but in retrospect, she realises she should have been. At the time, stupidly, she thinks that Richard isn't the type to play around. As if there is a type.
- You think there isn't?
- All walks of life, remember.
- You don't have to believe every report you read.
- Anyway, as Anna makes the insinuation, completely innocently, Richard feels he needs to defend himself. Like you did just now.
- I thought we were talking about your novel.

- How are you?
- All right. You?
- You don't seem all right.
- It feels wrong.
- What?
- The novel.
- ?
- All I'm sure of is the starting image. Nothing else.
- Which image?
- Sunday evening, two people, a man and a woman, in their mid-fifties standing in the kitchen. The woman has cooked dinner. The man has had a bath and has come down, in his jeans and a clean shirt, hair freshly washed. He's opening a bottle of wine, as he does every Sunday. The kitchen is large and they are standing a few metres apart. At the point when he is holding the bottle in between his knees and pulling out the cork, which is almost out, at that exact

57

point – I see him using one of those old-fashioned cork screws, he is leaning forward – the woman says: we won't need the wine tonight. He looks up; he doesn't know why she says that. As it happens, neither does she. His first thought is that wine doesn't go with what she has cooked. He wants to ask whether she would prefer beer. But he doesn't say it. There is a silence, a palpable silence between them. Half a minute, or less, but when they look back on that evening, the silence will seem very long. They both sense something is going to happen. Something is going to be said that will change their lives for good. That's all I had. I didn't know what was going to happen, what either of them had done or what's about to be said.

– I see.
– I also know that later the woman was to be struck by her words. She couldn't explain where they came from. Some strange force spoke on her behalf.
– The woman's sixth sense.
– Only a man would believe that.
– Your readers would.
– Well, they aren't getting it spelt out by me. I'm not here to confirm their patriarchal prejudices.
– What are you here for?
– I don't know. I don't want to think about it. Not today. Not after the day I've had.
– Sorry.
– – Anna has read a lot about memory; Anna knows that memory can be deceptive and therefore when she looks back she is aware that the moment in the kitchen looks momentous, theatrical almost only in retrospect – as if the two of them were on the stage in a second rate melodrama,

an inferior *Who's Afraid of Virginia Woolf* – and it may not have been like that at the time.

– – And then?

– I don't know. To start with, I had no idea what happened between those two people, what caused the drama that follows, the nitty-gritty of it didn't interest me. I even wrote a short story where it's never revealed what happened. The woman talks about those five words her husband used and the whole story is about the impact on her, the surprise, how she didn't know her husband well enough to expect him to say those five words but the reader never finds out what they are. At the same time, I was trying to imagine what could have happened and the most obvious thing would have been that one of them has had an affair. Since that's the most obvious, I didn't want to use it. Then I happened to be reading about prostitution, there's been so much in the papers, and I wondered what it would be like if the man had actually told his wife that he had been seeing prostitutes.

– And then you started researching the topic?

– Yes, I began to wonder what would have happened.

– Hang on. But you never use that image of the two of them in the novel.

– No. Once I got the story going it didn't work. The image spurred me to come up with the story but it isn't part of it. I wanted the reader to be aware of what Richard is up to for a while, that is, before Anna knows. You remember that he keeps meaning to tell but is too scared.

– I don't blame him.

– He deserves to get hell.

– A matter of opinion.

- What do you mean?
- She should have been more reasonable.
- Reasonable? You have no idea how a woman feels in that situation. No man should preach to me about that.
- All right.
- Is that all you can say?
- I'm sorry. No need to get so angry. Back to Richard, please.
- Okay. Something always happens and he doesn't tell her. He's looking for an opportune moment, hoping to mitigate her reaction. At some point he plans to make a nice dinner, or take her out, make her feel good but then he thinks it inappropriate: a parody of proposing in a restaurant.
- Poor Richard.
- It didn't just happen to him. Nor was it a one off. He actively sought the women for eight years.
- Okay, but I can imagine his fear of her temper. She's a strong and impulsive woman.
- You mean he needs a placid wife who would take his news calmly.
- No, he was foolish but I feel for him.
- You identify with him?
- No. I sympathise with him. Not the same.
- Because you have experienced my anger.
- As you say, this isn't about us.
- I don't know any more.
- It's not about us!
- If you say so.
- What do you mean? You're the author.
- In a way.
- In a way?
- Well, things happen and I use them. We are both authors

of things that happen.
- So it is about us.
- ?
- Is it about us?
- What do you think?
- I hope not.
- So do I.
- Look, let's leave it. I'd rather know about Richard.
- ?
- I'm sorry if I upset you. Please, tell me.
- Eventually, he decides to prepare her favourite food at home. When he gets in, he finds a note: Anna has gone to collect their younger daughter from the station. The daughter is arriving with a friend who is interested in doing research in Richard's field of interest. He's furious. Their younger daughter always turns up unannounced. He spends the weekend with them in a terrible state of anxiety. He and Anna try to make love but he can't. That is the first time it's ever happened to him with her. Anna tries to help by playing it down, attributing it to his tiredness.
- It's so false when women do that.
- What else are they supposed to do?
- Depends. I don't know. But tell me, what next?
- They are lying on the bed, after failing to have sex, their heads are next to each other. He thinks how strange it is to be so close, their brains separated only by skin and a bit of bone and yet she can't tell what's on his mind. He finds that comforting: at least some privacy for his dreadful secret.
- Anna strikes me as a character who never seems to know, let alone care, what Richard's feeling.

- Are you trying to say that I don't care what you are feeling?
- Not at all.
- Are you sure?
- This is not about us; I thought we'd established that.
- ?
- What about Richard?
- He only tells her when he has no choice, once he's been sacked from his job and fears the case might be in papers.

꧁

- Good day?
- Not bad. Making progress. Slowly. And you?
- Nothing to report.
- You always say that.
- It's true.
- Are you afraid I might use what you tell me? Something about your colleagues?
- No.
- Good.
- Well, yes. I am.
- Don't be silly. I wouldn't create problems for you.
- Of course not. Who was around today?
- Tanya.
- Tell me.
- I was wondering how she got to where she is.
- You mean why she's a prostitute.
- Yes.
- And?
- She was brought up by her mother. Poor, working class background.

- Which part of the country?
- I haven't decided yet. She lives in Birmingham when she goes to the consciousness-raising group. I would say she was raised somewhere in the West Midlands. Wolverhampton perhaps, or Coventry. Something like that. Is it important?
- I was just wondering.
- I'm not the type of novelist who likes to work out the characters' entire CVs.
- As a reader, sometimes one wants to know.
- As for Tanya, while she's growing up, her mother takes casual jobs from time to time. Tanya only remembers one holiday ever. A week in Blackpool. Lots of rain and wind but they went to the beach every day and every day she had an ice-cream.
- I can smell abuse.
- A couple of times her mother had a headache and stayed in their room in a bed and breakfast. Tanya, eight at the time, was taken out by a friend of her mother's, an elderly man. She remembered him as kind. He bought her presents, allowed her to choose them herself. She remembers having a bracelet and a ring. A candy stick as well.
- Has he got a name?
- Actually, he has. He's Marvin.
- How did you come up with that? We don't know anyone of that name. Sounds American.
- It seemed right for the image I have of him. And he isn't American.
- What does he look like?
- A retired working class man. Early sixties, slim, with a lined face and dark brown hair, possibly dyed. He's gentle

and seems kind and doesn't think he's doing anything wrong putting his hand inside Tanya's blouse.

- Is that what he does? Nothing more?
- Oh, no. He asks her whether she's warm enough and puts his hand on her chest to check. His fingers are cold and bony and she doesn't like him touching her but she's too shy to say anything to an adult. When they pass by the guest house where he is staying, they go in because he needs to get something he's forgotten. In the room he asks her whether she would like to have a rest. She doesn't—
- Wouldn't he insist?
- No. Absolutely not.
- Okay, it's your decision.
- They leave and return to the promenade.
- I hope you're not describing the promenade.
- I am.
- How can you without seeing it?
- Done my research. Looked at pictures. Read about it.
- Clichés.
- Isn't the whole point of Blackpool that it's a cliché: the working class holiday?
- What do you know about the working class? Done your research?
- Look. This isn't a documentary. I'm writing a fictional story. I have imagination.
- I know you do.
- What's that supposed to mean?
- That you're a writer. A novelist. Have imagination.
- Sometimes I wonder whether I should be telling you all this.
- Why not? I thought I'd been helpful.

64

- Some of the time. But it's not only that.
- Then what?
- This need that I have to show you what I'm doing, to get your feedback; it makes me feel insecure, unsure of what I've written.
- Why do you say that?
- In the past, whenever I felt unhappy with something, I carried on regardless. Now, it's as if I need constant feedback, perhaps even approval.
- Are you finding this one harder than the others?
- I think so.
- Why?
- I don't know. This story makes me question our own life, our marriage. Makes me insecure in more ways than one.
- Isn't that a normal part of the creative process?
- You could say that, but the problem is that it makes the novel different from the one I'd like to write. I don't know how to write about this subject.
- Write about something else. See what happens, where it takes you. I've heard you tell others that.
- Yes, but I'm too hooked on the subject; I really want to address it. I can't let go. The most frustrating feeling is that whatever I write about Anna's suffering, I'm faced with the impossibility of conveying the horror she experiences.

※

- You didn't finish telling me about Tanya.
- You mean after Blackpool.
- Yes.
- Well, that man—

- Marvin?
- Yes, and a few others, kept taking her out and buying her trinkets. At the time she was thinking it was wonderful but as she hit her early teens they started touching her more intimately, putting their cold hands into her knickers, saying they were making sure if she was warm enough. At fifteen, she slept with several of them. Each called himself her boyfriend and at the time that's what she thought they were. She left school—
- No qualifications.
- Yes—
- What do you mean, yes, she had some or yes, she didn't?
- She had none so she took a job in a bar. For a while it was okay, then the publican tried to have sex with her and she left. She worked in a fair ground and then in another pub where she met Dave. He was only a couple of years older than her and when he bought her a drink and asked her out, she felt he was a real boyfriend. Not like those old men who, she found out later, had been giving money to her mother.
- Her mother was pimping her?
- Yes, and Dave soon got in on the act too. He would bring a friend and spin a story about how the friend was lonely, his girlfriend had left him and so on and would ask Tanya to give him a cuddle. She didn't want to but he pleaded with her and so she did. And then she was left alone with yet another friend and he raped her. Dave claimed it was all a misunderstanding and that it wouldn't happen again. But it did. She left him. He came back, promised that it would be just the two of them. Soon she was pregnant. She has a child—

- Whose child is it?
- Dave's, I suppose. I don't intend to make much of it. He doesn't really care except when the child cries and he blames Tanya.
- I see.
- Soon after she has a child, he forces her to go on the street. That's when she comes into the story.
- Rather cliché, I'm afraid.
- I know. True stories of prostitutes are often cliché.
- True? Tanya's?
- Yes, a compilation based on accounts I've read.

⁂

- Good day?
- Yes. Yours?
- Fine. Tell me about Anna.
- She's about to give up Rachel.
- The therapist?
- Yes.
- Why?
- She feels it's not working.
- In what way?
- She wants answers. She wants to know why Richard visited prostitutes.
- Not for the therapist to tell her.
- Anna wants to know what's wrong with her. Why did he not want her?
- But he did. They still had a sex life.
- Then why others?
- Are you asking me? You're the writer.

- You're a man.
- But not the man.
- Are you sure?
- What are you saying?
- Oh, forget it.
- ?
- So, why did Richard go to others? What do you think?
- As a novelist, you should come up with the answer.
- But I can't think why a man in Richard's position would pay for sex in real life.
- I thought your books weren't about real life.
- No, not in the sense of mimesis but in this novel the causes of behaviour and the reasons behind actions of the characters aren't different from real life.
- Does it mean that you expect your readers to learn from this novel how to behave in similar situations?
- No, well, yes but I don't like the way you put it.
- Okay, you want them to think prostitution is iniquitous?
- Oh, yes. Definitely.
- And if a female reader found herself in the same situation as Anna, do you think your novel would be helpful to her?
- Perhaps. I'd be glad if it did but that's not why I'm writing it.
- Why are you writing it?
- Not sure any more.

❧

- Haven't I heard this music before?
- You're back early.
- Have I surprised you?

- No.
- I think I have.
- Don't look so smug. I thought you said you'd be late.
- Well, I'm back.
- Good.
- I'm back and so is your Frenchman.
- ?
- Your Frenchman is back. Why would you be listening to his music?
- I've always liked it.
- Because it makes you think of Gustave.
- Don't be ridiculous.
- Where has it come from?
- Sarah got it for me a few months ago.
- You never told me about it.
- Didn't I?
- You must have forgotten to mention it.
- I must have.
- Is that why you listen to it when I'm not here?
- I can't believe you would think something like that, let alone say it.
- Okay. Let's say you aren't in touch but he gave you the CD. Posted it. For old times' sake.
- He disappeared from my life a year before I met you. I haven't heard from him since.
- Until now.
- Don't. Don't smile.
- Well, the love of my wife's life is back and I should not rejoice?
- He isn't back.
- He is back in your thoughts.

- Look, you don't deserve an explanation but I'll give it to you anyway.
- Go ahead.
- I've been working on Anna's therapy sessions. I've been thinking of my own experience. As you know, I had therapy to deal with that loss. So I remembered him. I remembered Casals' cello recording we used to listen to and I remembered that a few months ago Sarah bought me the CD, the new one, the digitally remastered version.
- Why would she do that?
- Recently released.
- But why this music?
- She's a friend. My best friend. She can buy me presents.
- But why this one except to remind you of your Frenchman?
- Because I've always liked the music.
- And the memories it brings.
- And the memories it brings if you like.

- Have you got the ending?
- What do you mean?
- What happens to Richard and Anna? Do they part or stay together?
- Not sure. What do you think?
- I think they should part.
- Why?
- Because they are not good for each other.

- I've given them two daughters.
- What a surprise.
- Don't worry, they're not called Emma and Ursula.
- The girls will be disappointed to have missed a chance to be famous.
- Don't be sarcastic.
- What about Bob?
- What about him?
- Is he still Bob?
- He still has his bobbishness but he is called Rob.
- You can't be serious.
- Why not?
- It's the same. They'll know.
- It's not the same. Sounds different.
- Comes from the same name.
- A very different image.
- Who says?
- I do. The sound or Rob or Robert conjures very different images from that of Bob.
- To you.
- Yes, to me. Doesn't it to you?
- No. Nor to my colleagues in the department.
- They must be poor readers.
- I don't care what kind of readers they are.
- Bob is so much better for what I need but as a concession to you—
- I'm grateful.

❧

- I have to use something else from our lives—

- Oh, no.
- Don't be paranoid. I was going to talk to you first.
- I'm not looking forward to that.
- You're not being supportive.
- Just don't tell me Richard has been appointed professor of politics specialising in women and political parties.
- Nowhere near as good as a history prof specialising in suffragettes.
- I told you it's too close.
- Stop worrying. But there is something from my own life that I have to use. It seems so obvious but I thought you may feel uncomfortable about it.
- She's into sex games—
- Gosh. No!
- He likes his nipples squeezed.
- Don't be silly. Too intimate to reveal.
- Thank God for that. So, what is it?
- You know when I was in therapy, I suffered from an obsession.
- Yes.
- All I could think about was that he had rejected me and had chosen a life without me, a life with another woman. I compared myself to them all the time. For obvious reasons, I thought he was with a French woman, and whenever I saw a French woman, I regarded her as a rival, I hated her. But the real problem was my feminism; women were meant to be my sisters. I couldn't admit it to anyone apart from Sarah. She understood how I felt and she was helpful but there came a point when she couldn't do anything more for me. She said I needed a professional. I went to Ruth.
- Ruth? Not Rachel?

- No, Ruth. Anna goes to Rachel. Anyway, I've been looking at my notes from those days. I seem to have been angry and sometimes hostile to Ruth and after a year, around the time when I met you, I walked out. Ruth didn't want me to. I said I feared getting too dependent on her. Ruth laughed. You're not a person who gets dependent on anyone, she said. Of course, I wasn't really afraid of that. I made it up because it sounded like the sort of thing a therapist would understand. The real reason was that I was bored with her. I could see where she was going. I could tell what she wanted me to say. I'd read Freud and Lacan, and Kristeva, I could see through her. It always puzzles me how those clever people in Woody Allen films have therapy for decades and don't get bored.
- Perhaps they do but they haven't much else. No one else to talk to.
- When I walked out on Ruth, I believed I could help myself.
- Did you help yourself?
- I think so. At the time it helped finding you and the knowledge that you wanted me. In the long term, it was the writing that helped.
- I wasn't much use long-term.
- I didn't say that.
- No, I suppose not, but it sounded like it.
- It doesn't work like that. It was only my illusion that I needed another man to get over the Frenchman.
- Now you know that you could never get over Gustave.
- I didn't say that.
- But it's true.
- I'm not answering that. What I want to tell you is that I see Anna in the same situation. She needs therapy but it

doesn't work for her, it doesn't give her what she wants. She believes she can help herself.
- By screwing around?
- What a crude thing to say. Typical of you to give advice to Richard and castigate Anna. What a biased reader you're.

⚶

- I need your help.
- The help of a biased, male reader?
- Yes.
- You must be really lost.
- That's not a kind thing to say to a writer.
- Isn't it?
- Definitely not. What would it do for my self-confidence?
- I didn't mean anything.
- Why did you say it then?
- I don't know. A joke.
- Wasn't funny. A facetious, careless sentence.
- Sorry, I didn't think—
- No, you didn't think. You never do.
- Look, I'm sorry. You seem to be touchy today.
- Telling me I'm lost. Of course I'm touchy.
- You say it all the time.
- That's different.
- Ah, one rule for you, another one for me.
- Don't be silly. How you never understand anything.
- What was it you wanted to ask?
- Nothing. Forget it.
- Don't be like that.

- Look, I'm sorry about before. I really am sorry. Please, let's talk.
- What about?
- You wanted to ask me something. You said I could help. I would like to.
- I'm not sure.
- Please.
- Okay. I don't know what to do about Richard's sexual background.
- Sexual background. Meaning?
- His early sexual awakening. I don't mean the actual sex, that as well, but before, his first awareness of sexuality.
- Do you need that?
- I think so. Therapists often look into it. Some of the causes of later problems often lie in the earliest experiences.
- I can only tell you about mine.
- And you fear that I'll use it.
- I don't mind; what I remember is fairly run of the mill.
- Tell me.
- Haven't I told you before? Masturbating and the like?
- Everyone does that. I'm more interested in the context.
- You mean looking at lingerie catalogues? Not that I ever saw one at home; boys at school passed them around.
- Yes, but not only that.
- I don't know what else.
- I seem to remember that once you mentioned something about your mother's aversion to the word penis—
- Ah yes, there was a documentary on television and this doctor mentioned the word and my mother—

- Walked out—
- Yes, but only after she switched off the television.
- Quite a scene. Didn't anyone protest? Your father?
- No one said anything. We were supposed to have felt ashamed.
- Ashamed at hearing the word?
- Yes.
- You never used the word at home.
- Lots of people still don't—
- I suppose you're right. I remember the girls' friends talking of front bottoms and the like. Unbelievable.
- I can see Anna teaching her daughters the Latin terms. You wouldn't fail to make her do that.
- Of course.
- And Richard feeling uncomfortable.
- Did you feel uncomfortable?
- No, not really. Just not used to it. Rather, I wasn't used to it for a long time.
- Richard's mother could make a scene when someone on television says penis. You don't mind, do you?
- I suppose not.
- Should Richard feel guilty each time he masturbates?
- I think so.
- Did you feel guilty?
- Of course I did and I worried that my mother might discover the stuff on my pyjamas. I would sponge it off but then they would be wet and that could be suspicious. I remember more than once deliberately spilling tea on them at breakfast so that I could put them in the wash.
- In twenty-five years of marriage, we never talked about you spilling tea on your semen stains. Isn't that strange?

- I don't know. It's not the sort of thing that crops up.
- I think it's strange. Richard's also likely to have things in his past that he never mentioned to Anna.
- But does it matter? It seems pretty insignificant to me. Only a psychologist would make a meal out of it.
- I agree. It matters only in so far as it shows the two of you as people who don't like talking about personal things.
- I'm not like Richard. I don't like when you say that.
- Sorry.
- It's the other way round. He's like me. And whose fault is that? You keep turning him into me.
- But you said you didn't mind as there was nothing unique about your earliest sexual awareness. Run of the mill – your words.
- I don't mind that. But you've taken other things from me.
- Nothing significant.
- Maybe not to you.
- You know what I've been thinking?
- No.
- How come you didn't mind talking about your personal experience this time?
- It felt as if I was talking about someone else.
- ?
- The chap I was then feels distant, alien. As if it had been someone else.
- I often have that feeling.
- Of separate selves?
- Of not much continuity between all those past selves and who I feel I am today.
- But what happened to all those past selves would have made you what you are now—

- The links and the continuity aren't obvious. Bringing that about, making a story, that's what I do to my characters.
- Maybe. I was thinking how Richard finds it difficult to see the point of revealing personal, intimate details. I think that's why he has an aversion to therapy.

※

- Good day?
- Fine. And yours?
- Nothing to report. I have a question: is Richard an addict?
- Depends on who you believe.
- Tell me.
- Not now.

※

- Hello.
- Hello.
- I've had a thought—
- Yes?
- I was wondering whether she could be rather demanding when it comes to sex.
- What are you getting at?
- Just wondering if she—
- Some men may like it—
- The woman being demanding?
- Yes. Don't you think?
- Does Richard like her being demanding?
- I didn't say she was.
- You're the author. You should be able to tell.

- I don't know. I'm not the kind of author who worries about such details.
- It's hardly a detail in this kind of novel.
- Not the way I look at it.
- You see, some men may like it but others might feel inadequate.
- Once again the male reader is supporting the male character.
- Think about it: prostitutes, particularly the type that he chooses – poor, uneducated, working-class women – they don't make him feel inadequate. That's why he goes to them.
- That's too neat. You're looking for reasons to blame her.
- It makes sense.
- To blame her?
- No, I meant him feeling inadequate with her.
- Even if that were so, it's only his feeling. She can't be responsible for that.
- She could help him feel more comfortable.
- She does.
- I doubt it. I bet she finds sex with him inadequate.
- Not at all. In fact, she feels that over the years he's become more adventurous. When they first met, he preferred lights out, the missionary position, lie back and think of England.
- Oh, so he has improved then.
- Definitely.
- I'm pleased to hear that. As for Anna, wouldn't her mother's perfectionism, high expectations, present a problem? Make her feel inadequate?
- Quite the contrary. It spurred her on. She was an exceptional student. Wrote her PhD in record time.

- I see. She's wonderful.
- Don't be sarcastic.
- But she never learned to be compassionate.
- As always, you're too harsh on her. One thing Anna does reveal to Rachel about her upbringing is that her mother never smiled, rarely praised her.
- A classic case of a person who has difficulties making and keeping friends.
- Where did you get that from?
- Common knowledge.
- And wrong. As you know, Anna has lots of friends, lots of clever friends.
- Aren't most of her friends male?
- So what?
- Just shows.
- Shows what?
- They aren't real friends; they're after her.
- You're being ridiculous.
- Colin, Maximilian, then that architect at her dinner party and even Mark.
- They may find her attractive but it doesn't mean they're after her.
- Not the impression I get.
- Anyway, there is Sarah.
- Well, that friendship goes through a deal of strain.
- Of course it does but they've known each other for thirty years and have stayed close. They are loyal to each other, and when one of them needs support, she knows she can get it from the other. When Sarah's partner Jocelyn died of breast cancer—
- The cello player?

- That's right.
- I still wonder why you need such detail. You keep saying you aren't writing a social realist text and yet—
- I don't know. It seemed right. Maybe a reader will come up with a pattern, a link, something that makes sense.
- That's always possible.
- Anna thinks of Jocelyn every now and then. At some point she remembers Jocelyn's funeral, a bright, sunny, freezing day. All crispy. Another time she remembers the music and how Jocelyn had it all ready as soon as she got the prognosis. Anna thinks of particular pieces—
- Did they play your Frenchman's stuff?
- What's the matter with you?
- Just wondering. Why wouldn't they play that? You always say how wonderful it is.
- And so it is.
- To me, mentioning this seems superfluous detail. Jocelyn is a distraction. No function in the plot. I thought you preferred stylized writing. Not mimetic.
- You can't judge it unless you read the whole novel. Some of the details are symbolic.
- I'll take your word for it.
- While Anna helps Sarah at the time of Jocelyn's death, and for months afterwards, Sarah is there for her. It's a very strong, supportive relationship. But Anna's friendships with men are different. Those men, they like having a vivacious and intelligent female friend. She is sociable and open and that appeals to them
- You too have quite a few male friends.

☙

- Good day?
- So so. Yours?
- Fine.
- I've been thinking of Richard's mother.
- Yes?
- Starting with that scene you described when your mother—
- I thought you were talking about Richard's mother.
- Let me finish. I used that idea, that situation you mentioned when your mother was offended at the word 'penis' on television, and it made me think of other events in his life. I have this chapter where he remembers, see, it's him, not you, where he remembers making love to Anna for the first time.
- In a room in an old hotel? And saving a spider afterwards?
- No. Silly you. I can make things up. Richard has a small car. His first one. They drive to the countryside and have a picnic in a field of wild flowers. It's a bright and warm, late spring afternoon. They've eaten and they lie on a blanket, side by side. Anna watches the clouds, large puffy things, like scoops of whipped cream, and suggests that they make up stories about them.
- Wow, we've never done that.
- No, because we are not them.
- Glad to hear it.
- So, for Anna, each cloud has an identity. She sees a Buddhist monk, Druids, particular Elizabethan actors, and a whole series of famous paintings. Richard is both amused and lost. What can he offer? All he can see are thick white clouds drifting across the blue sky. He loves her confidence and imagination and longs to be part of that world. For now, he is an alien but maybe she could be his ticket. He

feels love and warmth for her. Later, he worries that those feelings were mainly envious self-interest borne out of the hope that he could be like her.

- Poor Richard. You don't think you're patronizing him?
- No. Do you want to hear the rest or not?
- Okay.
- He kisses her frantically and she responds. They half undress each other and he suggests that if they move to the car, he could cover the windows and they could make love. She stops and stares at him. For a moment, he worries that he was being presumptuous. She says: but why not here? It's so beautiful. He's taken aback by her directness. Someone might see us, he says. There's no one around, she laughs.
- Oh, Richard.
- He's surprised when she doesn't mind undressing in bright sunshine and as he watches her, comfortable in her nakedness, he admires and fears her.
- I am sure twenty-five years later he still feels the terror that he felt then, that terror that he may not live up to her expectations.
- That's beside the point. We are in a flashback. Focus on that. So, while they are making love for the first time, he can't stop worrying that someone might turn up. He can even hear his mother: you should be ashamed of yourself, Richard. You have betrayed me.
- Wow. That's scary.
- Or could he feel his mother sitting on his shoulder . . . would that be too much?
- He'd better tell his therapist about it. Or his orthopaedic consultant.

- Do you mind if I use Mary Carleton?
- Use Mary Carleton?
- Don't tell me you've forgotten who she was.
- No. Of course not.
- So, is that okay?
- Okay for what?
- To use her in the novel. Do you mind?
- You mean, describe me asking you out?
- For a coffee.
- Are you saying that's how Anna and Richard meet?
- Why not?
- Because it's ours. Between you and me. No one knows about it.
- Exactly, no one knows about it. No one will be able to tell that it's us.
- I'd prefer it to remain private.
- But it is private. It won't be associated with us.
- Other people don't meet or get interested in each other because one of them is talking about a seventeen-century woman.
- How do you know?
- Unlikely.
- Besides, she wasn't just any seventeenth-century woman.
- I know she was special, special to you.
- And she is special to Anna. Anna tells Richard about her, explains the idea of self-fashioning.
- Nothing's sacred to you. You pilfer our lives for whatever you need.
- Darling, don't be stubborn. I really need this one.

- You say that about everything. I've heard it so many times.
- This one shouldn't be controversial.
- I'm sure you can think of a better one.
- Not really. I've tried, believe me. You see, Anna and Richard meet for the first time at a birthday party. That doesn't feature in the story but he refers to it in a flashback. The second time they see each other, she's coming out of the university library, he's going in. Their paths cross on the big steps outside, overlooking the green with the clock tower. Now, that's not Bristol. That's Birmingham. That's not us.
- Thank God for small mercies.
- He's pleased to see her. Presumably, she feels the same but we get the memory from his point of view.
- So, you assumed I was pleased to see you.
- Weren't you?
- Yes, I was.
- You see, I was right.
- But I don't like him copying me. It feels as if he's taking over my life.
- Don't be silly. You're not Richard.
- I'm becoming him.
- Are you?
- I can't help it.
- Don't say that.
- You're driving me there.
- Is there something you want to tell me?
- ?
- Have you copied him in . . . other things?
- No, well, yes. No, you have copied me to make him.
- Are you like him or not?

- We need to get out of this. I feel in a bind.
- Okay. But I need Carleton: it occurs to him that Anna could be persuaded that self-fashioning, inventing different identities, is important for men too and that by being Alan, Alan Roberts, he was self-fashioning himself, he was, if you like, re-enacting his darker side, his fantasy.
- That's stretching it a bit.
- Of course, but he's desperate. And so he develops the idea – which he hopes Anna might buy – the idea that Richard always loved his wife and Richard could never do wrong, it was only Alan, his darker side.
- I can't see the point.
- It gives him temporary comfort, hope that he can sort it out, at least at home.
- It also makes him look stupid.
- Possibly but he's a desperate man. And a desperate man is prone to self-delusion. Can you see now why I need the Carleton discussion? I need to introduce her as a symbol of self-fashioning?
- You could still use the word but it could come out of some other situation.
- Not as good as Carleton.
- Carleton was also a cheat and a liar, a very clever one. He's a cheat and a liar, but not a clever one.
- This is the first time you've said something bad about him.

৵৶

- Good day?
- Yes. We're getting there. You?
- Nothing special. How's my alter ego?

- Who?
- Richard?
- He is not your alter ego.
- You behave as if he were.
- I hope not. I wouldn't like to be his partner.
- What's happening to him?
- He has a new therapist.
- I thought he was set against therapy.
- Well, he has no choice and gradually he accepts that it would be good to have someone to talk to.
- What's he like? Assuming it's a he.
- Stuart. Early forties, divorced. Dreams of being a writer and undertakes therapy training to support himself while writing a novel. Believes that listening to the stories of his clients might spur his imagination. That doesn't mean he isn't serious about helping Richard. In fact, he believes what Richard needs is a male friend, a confidant, and while he would be overstepping his professional boundaries if he let their relationship develop into friendship, he's confident he can at least offer a listening ear and be a non-judgmental companion.
- He doesn't follow any specific method? No Twelve Steps?
- No Twelve Steps, definitely not. In fact, Richard asks about it when he first contacts the therapist. Stuart reassures him that his work is based on cognitive behaviour therapy.
- Trendy.
- Yes.
- As far as I understand the method, it means Richard has to face the situations that in the past would have led him to contact prostitutes but, in a safe environment, with the therapist's help, he has to develop different ways of

reacting.
- Exactly.
- What are those situations in Richard's case?
- Being sexualised on the train.
- Okay, that's straightforward. What else?
- Situations that contribute to his low self-esteem.
- Such as?
- For example, when Anna makes him feel inadequate.
- Oh, so you admit she does?
- Yes, but it's not her fault.
- ?
- It's the way he takes it.
- Give me something specific.
- For example, when Anna disagrees with him.
- You mean when she dismisses his views.
- I wouldn't use that word. Too judgmental.
- Okay. What do they disagree about?
- Art, for example. She feels that's her area and he has what she considers somewhat set, old-fashioned views. But more importantly, they tend to differ on domestic decisions, such as home décor. She maintains he has no visual sense.
- Meaning that his visual sense is different from hers.
- If you put it like that.
- Richard has inherited that from me.
- True of most men unless they are architects or artists.
- A sexist comment.
- Based on experience.
- Still sexist. You tend to overrule me when it comes to home decor—
- Hang on, I was talking about them, not us.
- Your attitude might have a damaging effect on me; it might

bring about my low self-esteem.
- Why is it that each time we talk about my writing, you turn it into a discussion about you?
- For obvious reasons. I can't tell anymore where I end and Richard begins.
- You're exaggerating.
- I haven't mentioned it to you, but I had a dream recently about your novel.
- Really?
- Your publisher didn't want it. They didn't say why, or rather, that question never came up. And your agent tried elsewhere. And no one would have it.
- Thanks for that. Makes me feel really good.
- Sorry, it was only a dream—
- A nightmare, more likely.
- For you, yes, but, I'm sorry to say I was relieved.
- Great.
- It's obvious why, isn't it?
- Your bloody unconscious desire. Do you know what it does to my confidence as a writer? I have to live with the fear that no one will want what I write and I try to push it to the back of my mind, but it's always there.
- I don't want it to happen. Of course not. But the dream shows how uncomfortable I'm with being turned into Richard.
- You are not Richard. He visited prostitutes for eight years.

- I miss Tanya.
- You miss the young prostitute?

- Yes.
- ?
- Sometimes I think she comes across as a more sympathetic character than either of the other two.
- My writing has never been about creating sympathetic characters.
- I know. I wonder what happened to her?
- She's in the centre of Birmingham, trying to steal some clothes. A t-shirt actually.
- And?
- She doesn't manage. She gets cold feet.
- Thank God for that.
- Who knows, it might be good for her to get caught. Someone might help her. A social worker or someone. The reader could see her attempt at stealing as a call for help. But perhaps it's much simpler: she has very little money and can't afford to buy what she wants. One of the women who works with her boasts that she steals most of her clothes and encourages Tanya to do the same. Tanya manages to take a lipstick, but it's only a sample and she hates herself for that. She thinks how she has always been a failure. At school, teachers thought she was useless and now she can't even nick a new lipstick. She throws the lipstick into a rubbish bin and, in the process, accidentally drops her purse on the ground. It's picked up by Anna, Anna in her mid-twenties, of course—
- Wow, that busybody finding herself at the right place and the right time.
- There is another woman with Anna and they run after Tanya to return it to her. Anna recognises Tanya and asks if she wants to come to the group again. We're going there

now, she says. Tanya has no intention of joining them but
something prevents her from saying it. As before, at the
sight of Anna, she becomes tongue-tied. What is it with
this woman, she thinks. Why does she do this to me?
- Meaning Anna?
- Yes, and she remembers Sarah. They're always so bloody
  polite and sorry about everything and she can't cope with
  that.
- I can see how that would happen to a working class girl,
  even one who's street wise, next to a posh type like Anna.
- Yes, and it makes Tanya angry. Anyway, Anna introduces
  the woman who's with her. She's called Mary and she's
  recently joined the group. Mary works in a shoe shop.
  Now Tanya's interested: somebody in the group who isn't
  a student and there's also the shoe shop connection: Tanya
  always wanted to work in a shoe shop. She loves shoes.
- Wow. You and Tanya sharing something; that really is a
  surprise.
- I'm not the only one who loves good shoes.
- The only one I know. But I bet she hasn't got hundreds
  of pairs like you.
- Don't exaggerate. I don't.
- Well—
- Listen, back to the novel. Tanya sometimes goes in and
  tries on shoes purely for pleasure though she can see that
  sales assistants get annoyed with her. She imagines that
  if she worked there, she would love fetching boxes and
  helping customers try on the shoes. She wonders whether
  it would be a good idea to make friends with Mary and
  see if she could help her get a job in her shop. So she goes
  with the women despite a nagging voice telling her that

she shouldn't. On the way, Anna says that the group is thinking of organising social activities and Mary suggests bowling; she often goes with her work mates. Anna doesn't know; she's never been and so she asks Tanya what she thinks.

- One wouldn't expect Anna to know about bowling.
- Not everyone is into such things.
- She isn't because you aren't.
- So what?
- Nothing, only pointing out how much you've made Anna in your own image.
- As far as I'm concerned, life's too short—
- To waste on bowling.
- Exactly.
- The problem is that you look down upon those who don't share your view—
- That's my prerogative.
- And my prerogative as a reader is to point out the similarities between you and your protagonist.
- Sometimes you sound like those annoying readers who think everything is autobiographical.
- Not so far from the truth in this case.
- I'm married to you not to Richard.
- Changing a name here and there does not alter the rest.
- ?

❧

- You didn't finish telling me about Tanya.
- What do you want to know?
- She was in town and met Anna and some other woman

who works in a shoe shop. They were talking about bowling.

- Yes, that's right.
- Does the idea attract Tanya?
- Yes. She's been before with the women she works with, celebrating a birthday.
- I like Tanya.
- You keep saying that.
- She's the female character the reader would go for. Not Anna.
- Depends on the reader.
- What next?
- The three women go off together. When they arrive, the set-up is the same as before: a large table with a freshly baked cake in the middle, women making tea and coffee, photocopies of the article for the day lying around. Its title is 'Whores'; the author is Andrea Dworkin.
- Good old Dworkin. I remember you reading that stuff.
- To Tanya, the name doesn't mean anything and the title puzzles her. Are they going to talk about prostitution, she wonders. Once again, she finds most of the discussion incomprehensible. Someone says that the power of men in pornography is imperial power; Marcuse is mentioned and his notion of women as the land, men as the army, and several women refer to the phallus and its symbolic representation as the weapon—
- I bet she has no idea what's going on.
- Of course not. She listens amazed that everyone has so much to say and watches everyone scribbling, even Mary. Tanya has to pretend she's with them and pretending isn't difficult for her. That's what she does with the punters.

The discussion turns to the essentialism of patriarchal discourse which posits the whore as a whore by nature, the whore as born, and it takes a male to discover her as such. That makes men not predators but facilitators, a woman says, and then the question is how feminism could counter such discourse. A whore is born, some women are just like that, they enjoy being whores, another woman says, but others argue with her.

- Are you trying to make them sound pretentions?
- No, just giving the flavour of the group.
- You mean your group?
- Yes.
- Tanya should walk out. It's mad she has to listen to that.
- Well, she wonders whether she was born a whore. She thinks about those male friends of her mother and of Dave's friends, who were not really friends. Was she a whore before they came along? The discussion heats up and eventually Anna asks whether anyone in that room has ever known a prostitute or whether their views are just prejudice. Anna adds that prostitutes are our sisters and we should think how we can help them as they are the real victims of patriarchy.
- Well, she no longer believes in that.
- That's Richard's fault.
- Come on, in her fifties, she chooses to be hostile to prostitutes.
- She can't help it. Look, that's twenty five, thirty, years later. Let's stick to the chapter and the group. Most women agree with Anna, but several voices rise in opposition. The idea emerges that the group should invite a prostitute, a working woman, to speak to the group.

- So, Tanya comes out?
- Wait a minute. One woman suggests they could even apply for funds to pay a prostitute—
- Pay a prostitute?
- You know what I mean? For her time. A visiting speaker fee.
- Yes, I see.
- But, where can they find a prostitute?
- Right in front of them.
- Eventually, Tanya speaks and says that she knows one. Most women want to know whether the woman would be able to come to the group. Tanya says she could arrange it and that the woman wouldn't need payment. They go to a pub and over lunch with Anna, Sarah and—
- Well, she's a brave woman to go with them.
- She admits she works on the street. The women are stunned into silence and, for a moment, Tanya regrets coming out. When they speak, she thinks they're sorry for her and she tells them that she doesn't need their sympathy.
- Right, that's a change in attitude, her speaking up for herself.
- That's right. Telling them who she is gives her confidence.
- Anna apologizes; they've been patronizing. Before they part, they arrange for Tanya to speak to the group; Anna offers to have a place in the nursery for Lilla for the day.
- Is that from your consciousness-raising group?
- No.
- The cake and the articles?
- Yes, that's from us. But not Tanya; we never had anyone from outside the university. In fact, I don't think I would have cared for them to come. Anna's better than me.

- So she's your idealised younger self. She comes across as too perfect, I mean, in her young days. What happened? Why is she so horrible now?
- She isn't. But being with him would have had its effect.
- Oh, it's his fault.

⁂

- Good day?
- Okay, I think.
- You think? Who was it?
- Tanya.
- So, what happens?
- A year passes and Anna and Sarah are in a taxi on their way to a small arts cinema. As they drive past a park, Anna notices Tanya and a couple of other women standing by the roadside, under some trees. She stops the taxi and they get out. Needless to say, Tanya isn't pleased to see them but it's very cold and windy and she hasn't had any custom and when the two women suggest a drink, she thinks she might just as well go and warm up. If she gets any work, it would be more likely when the pubs close. They walk to a local; Tanya has a whisky. A couple of men approach their table; they know her.
- Does that make the other two uncomfortable?
- I don't think so. Anyway, Tanya tells them to push off; one of the men says: I see, now that you have your posh friends, we aren't good enough. The women ignore him. When Anna leaves the table to get more drinks and Sarah is in the toilet, Tanya notices Sarah's bag casually left on the chair. She takes twenty pounds out of her purse. Serves

her right, she thinks, stupid woman leaving her bag like that.

- Exactly. I'm with Tanya on that.
- Sarah won't miss it, Tanya reasons, whereas it might save her from Dave's blows when she gets home after a poor night.
- Well, she needs it more than they do. To each according to their need.
- Yes, but she's stealing.
- From the rich.
- They aren't rich.
- Compared to Tanya, they are.
- I suppose so. The two women again talk of the group, say that they have some new members from outside the university and that they're really keen to do more campaigning; they mention fund-raising for the women's refuge. What's that, Tanya asks.
- A good question; she may need to know about it.
- They tell her – she has never heard of a place like that – and they part, giving their number to her; they would love to keep in touch. She doesn't give them hers: no point, she lies, I'm about to move.
- I can imagine these busy bodies turning up at her house. She is wise not to give them her address.
- She fears what Dave might do if he saw them.
- I can see where this is going.
- Can you?
- He will beat her up and she will go to a refuge; the two women will help.
- Something like that. Gosh, am I making it too predictable?
- Not necessarily. But it's what I said before: the gun on

the table . . . The mention of the women's refugee has to have a point.

※

- Good day?
- I think so.
- You're not sure?
- I revisited a chapter. Tinkered with it.
- Which one?
- The difficult one. Most difficult.
- ?
- When he tells her.
- I hope you toned down her reaction.
- I couldn't do that.
- You're the author. You can do anything.
- It's a most horrible thing that he did and it wouldn't make sense to underplay it.
- She overreacts.
- Male—
- Reader. What else can I be?
- Make the effort to understand how she feels.
- I do, but her reaction's completely irrational.
- She's in shock.
- She could step back and think.
- I don't think so.
- Not straight away but after a few hours, the next day. But she doesn't.
- It takes longer than that to recover from such a revelation. If one can ever recover.
- She's impetuous.

- Me again. She got it from me.
- You said it.
- But seriously, you can't imagine any woman thinking rationally in that situation.
- I can. There are women who would stay calm and assess what's happened, think where to go next.
- Very few women would be able to do that. Certainly not Anna.
- That's her problem.
- You just don't understand how shocking it is.
- They're both alive and healthy and, if she loves him, she should be able to think how to move on.
- Look, this is how it goes: she comes in, a bit earlier than usual, around five. She's excited. She's had some good news: a producer has contacted her with an idea to make a television programme called From Nana to Nursery Girls – you know, Nana by Manet. He's her favourite painter—
- Surprise, surprise.
- And she thinks it's wonderful to have him in the title together with the Gallery's painting.
- Why does it have to be Manet?
- I'm not the only Manet fan.
- I wish you'd write something that has nothing to do with us. It's bloody annoying.
- I've only taken a few minor details.
- That's not what it feels like to me.
- Stop complaining. Wait until you see the whole thing. You won't even notice the details. The main issue has nothing to do with us.
- Who knows?
- What do you mean?

- Nothing. Just a joke.
- What did you mean when you said that?
- Nothing.
- Why did you say it then?
- One doesn't know what might happen to us, what's in store.
- Such as, you being like—
- I'm not saying that.
- What are you saying then?
- Nothing. Let's leave it for now.

❧

- How are you?
- Fine.
- How was your day?
- Fine.
- Look, I'm sorry about yesterday. I shouldn't have gone on. As you say, I need to wait and see the whole text.
- Okay.
- I was thinking about the difficult chapter.
- Yes?
- You said you've tinkered with it.
- Yes.
- You mentioned some good news, some television programme—
- Yes, that's why Anna is so chatty, excited, when she comes in. It takes her a while to register that something's wrong.
- Too self-centred, as always.
- That's unfair.
- She never notices when Richard has a problem.

- Look, I'm telling you about my novel. If you want to go on about us—
- Who was talking about us?
- You use every opportunity to criticize me.
- I was referring to Anna—
- And she's like me.
- In some ways.
- You see. You think she's like me and—
- Who made her so similar to you?
- I think she is wonderful and even if she's not perfect, she doesn't deserve what happens. No woman does.
- Okay.
- Okay.
- Look, I'm sorry.
- Fine.
- I'd like to hear what happens. Please?
- She's happy. Her enthusiasm, her passion, it all pours out and then in the middle of a sentence she notices his subdued face, his hunched body, his inability to share what she's talking about. She panics something has happened to the girls. He reassures her they're okay. She asks whether he's ill. He isn't. She says that whatever it is, they will get through it together. She loves him and he shouldn't worry, she will help him.
- If she could guess what it is, she wouldn't be saying it.
- How could she possibly guess? It would never have crossed her mind.
- And then he tells her.
- Yes, he says that they are getting rid of him at work.
- I'm trying to picture it. Where are they?
- In the lounge. He's sitting on the sofa, she's standing in

the middle of the room, facing him, but as soon as she notices the state he's in, she sits down next to him, takes his hand in hers.

- You make it sound like a play.
- That's how I see it. I need to visualise the scene to be able to write the dialogue.
- Right. And then?
- When she hears that they want to sack him, she is incredulous. She almost laughs. She relaxes visibly. You can't be serious, she says. You have the best RAE record. She mentions the Suffragette centre he founded and now directs, which has gained an international reputation as the best collection of the material on the Movement. Why would they want to get rid of you? He says: because I visited a prostitute.
- You mean, he says one prostitute, just the one?
- Yes, I think he would try to play it down.
- I see. That's changed.
- Yes.
- Anna would know that seeing a prostitute isn't a sackable offence.
- Perhaps but, as you can imagine, it doesn't cross her mind at the time. Let me read you what I wrote: we get Anna as the first-person narrator.
- Of course, as always in her sections.
- Here it goes: *We were in the kitchen. It was 6.55 on Sunday 13 November when I heard those words, those five words that came to constitute his revelation and when my body lost all sensation of weight and corporality and had anyone stuck a needle into my arm, or my leg, or indeed anywhere into my body, limbs or face, I would not have felt anything. The*

*words that my husband spoke, that sentence, that sentence that contained no more than five words, anaesthetised me. At the same time, my mind was emptied of everything that it had ever known or been aware of. Once the words were spoken, my conscious awareness of myself and of anything around me was obliterated to the point where the world around me was taken out of existence. I was standing in the kitchen without knowing that I was I; I was in the kitchen without knowing where I was. When my awareness of myself started coming back, and I began to have some notion, some notion of who I was, it was my surroundings and the man in front of me who seemed unknown, unreal even. It felt as if someone had placed white gauze between me and the space around, and this new world, this unknown world, a world in which I felt lost, this world appeared through a haze, like a dream. We were standing in a room that I had never seen and I had to screw up my eyes to try to find out where I was. The place looked like a kitchen, somebody's kitchen, some-body whom I didn't know and had never visited. I couldn't determine which colour and what material those worktops were made of; I tried to step nearer to see better, to touch the objects around me but my legs wouldn't move. I tried to stretch my arms but they seemed locked in place. I could hear humming and I remember thinking that it sounded like a fridge but my ears wouldn't let me determine where the noise was coming from. With my body paralysed and my mind in a state of amnesia, I should have felt calm but I didn't. Something somewhere inside me was trying to get out. I wanted to move but I couldn't. I wanted to speak but I couldn't. And who could I have spoken to, anyway? A few metres in front of me stood a man who looked exactly* like my husband and yet I knew, I was sure, he was not my husband. He was nothing like my husband. But why did he have the face shaped in the same way as that of my husband's and why was his body built in exactly the same way as the body of my husband, and why did his voice sound exactly the same as that of my husband? And when this man spoke, all I could think was how dare he speak to me and speak to me in the tone that suggested familiarity, how dare he call me by my first name? How dare he? His words had nothing to do with me and I didn't want to have anything to do with him. But where was my husband? This man looking at me and saying things that had nothing to do with me, things that I didn't want to hear, things that didn't make sense, who the hell was he, this usurper, this thief, this intruder? Had he murdered my husband and assumed his identity? I disliked that man and I wanted to make him go away. I wanted him to leave me alone but he stepped towards me and said my name. He was sorry. Sorry? What for? I didn't know him; I didn't want him to use my name. There was nothing to be sorry about. We were strangers who had never done anything together. Then came another sorry. And many more sorries. His sorries had nothing to do with me. And he called me by my name. And again. How dare he? I had to stop him. I wanted to scream, wanted to tell him to go away, I wanted to push him over. The bastard. More bloody sorry. And my name. My name. Stop it. Stop it. I wanted to shout but couldn't. The fool, the idiot – for what else could he be? – was sorry, sorry, sorry. He was sorry and then he said my name. My name. Again. I wanted to stop my ears. I wanted to cover them with both hands.

- Wow. No more screaming?

- No, that's the main change.
- Right. More powerful than her screaming.
- She doesn't explode as he expects her to. She implodes.
- I prefer that.
- I'm still not sure that I can communicate the enormity of the shock. I'll have to revisit it. Her growing irritation with him brings her back and once she comes back, she's angry.
- I can imagine her fury.
- She wants to know where Richard found the woman. He says he can't remember—
- He should stick with that.
- It wouldn't work. She insists and so he tells her about his e-mail account under a false name; she wants the password. He pleads with her not to look. She won't give in. Eventually, he tells her it's catandmouse13 - the year when the Cat and Mouse Bill, a notorious bill—
- Allowing the authorities to re-arrest a woman after she had been released from prison during a hunger strike . . .
- Well done.
- What do you expect, being married to a historian?
- Neat that, isn't it?
- What?
- Him using his specialist knowledge for his password and the irony of what the bill stood for and what the word means here: access to prostitutes.
- Most readers would miss it.
- Not all. You wouldn't.
- Come to think of it, quite funny that password.
- I don't think Anna finds it funny.
- That's her problem; she never sees the funny side of things.
- Don't be facetious.

- Perhaps in years to come, she'll look back and laugh at the absurdity of the password.
- I doubt it.
- You don't think time will heal—
- I don't know. But at the moment, it's hardly funny. She opens the account and finds hundreds of contacts.
- So he will have to admit there wasn't only one prostitute.
- Exactly.
- Your tinkering with the chapter: did you get rid of her demand?
- No. I think that's a very important part of Anna's psychology at that point.
- I thought you didn't go for character psychology.
- To some extent. In fact, I don't usually, but this novel demands it. It's very difficult to play linguistic and stylistic games with an issue such as prostitution, particularly if you are a woman.
- You're keeping that?
- Oh, yes. But I've altered it and added something else.
- What?
- Well, she looks up several of the women, stares at their images on websites, comments on their vulgarity, their cheapness. She sees their fees and services. She says she could do the same and better and she forces him to write her a cheque for a blow job. She demands £200 because she has a PhD. She says, you know, letters after the name make a difference. I don't think your whores had PhDs.
- Hell hath no fury—
- Reluctantly, he complies, writes her a cheque. They sit on the bed and she handles his penis but he can't get an erection—

- Hardly surprising under the circumstances.
- Your male empathy has no bounds. He wants to touch her breasts but she says that's extra. He asks her to put him in her mouth. I'm not putting this piece of flesh, this piece that's been in so many whores, I'm not putting it in my mouth without a condom, she says. He feels humiliated and he cries. They give up. And it's then she says she's no good, she needs to learn from a professional. He protests that she's great; she has nothing to learn from anyone. She insists that he arranges to meet his latest prostitute, and this time in a luxury hotel, and that he has sex with the woman while she watches. He's horrified but she says either he does that or he can move out.
- It's the same as before. I don't like that. She's mad. He shouldn't give in.
- He has no choice. Now Anna imagines the scene with the prostitute and Richard; in her mind it plays out as a scene in an Orson Welles film and she's sitting in an armchair, in a very large hotel room, smartly dressed, stilettos, an elegant cigarette in her hand, as she observes the action on the bed.
- What's the point of that?
- She's out of her mind.
- That's obvious.
- What I mean is that she's out of herself. Literally. She sees herself as someone else. That's her way of coping, playing a role.

- Good day.

- Not brilliant. Don't want to talk about it.
- Okay.
- And yours?
- The same as always.
- You always say that.
- It's always true.
- ?
- Something I wanted to say about Anna.
- Yes?
- In that crucial chapter, I think she's cruel. Cruel and insensitive. She can't hate him so much after she's loved him all those years.
- That bothers her too. No, that's not the right word. That worries her, frustrates her, drives her mad. But she can't help it. The way she sees it, he destroyed the identity of her husband, or who she believed he was. And he did the same to her. She's not who she thought she was.
- She's had a new experience.
- That's insulting.
- I grant you, a terrible experience, but still a new experience. She should learn from it, become a better person, more self-aware. More compassionate. Less judgmental. The opportunities are limitless.
- Maybe she will with time but for now, the shock's too big, too unsettling. Her politics, her feminism, her sisterly solidarity have been wiped out and she hates those women. Nor does she miss the irony that when she stares at the pictures of the women, she's judging them purely as objects, just like the punters do. And there's another irony: Richard was obsessed with the women. He couldn't organise a trip outside London, book the hotel, without checking out the

local women and contacting them, often booking them as well. Now she's obsessed; she can't tear herself away from the computer. She can't stop contacting them. She hates him for doing this to her.
- She's doing it to herself.
- He betrayed her. His deception hurts.
- People get over deception.
- It's not just deception, or betrayal for that matter. It's this destruction of certainty: who he is, this man she is married to, who she is, what kind of marriage they had. Nothing is as she thought it was. The whole map of Britain is dotted with names of women, like little pins with flags stuck all over the island. She can't hear of a place without thinking of the name of the woman Richard would have had there.
- You mean she knows exactly who he had where?
- More or less. She went through his emails and matched them with his and her diaries.
- Why does she want to know the details, the names?
- Part of her drive to find out why, why he did it.
- But she never finds out.
- There is no one answer. No neat way of explaining it.

⁂

- Who is this new woman? You called her Esther, didn't you?
- Yes. She's a six foot, fifteen stone, woman who operates from premises in several locations. One has a dungeon, specialising in S and M, another in dressing up.
- Is this made up or based on someone real? I hope you don't have problems with libel.

- A mixture of research and my imagination.
- Has Richard met her?
- No. To start with, he masturbated watching her thirty second video, but as they exchanged e-mails, some about mundane issues - such as Esther's car being stolen and the police not being very helpful - he stopped watching the recording. He thinks of her more as a virtual friend. Esther, however, is a business woman and she's beginning to think that Richard's one of those time-wasters who gets his kick from contacting escorts without ever booking. That's what she tells him in her latest message. He writes back, apologises and says that having never been with an escort, he—
- Liar.
- Absolutely. He likes to project the image of a virgin punter, someone who doesn't know how these things work. He says that he has a trip to Bruges coming up and wonders whether Esther could join him for the duration. He'd have to spend some time at the conference but for the rest, they could sample the delights of the city and test whether it's true that chocolate - for which Bruges is known, he stresses - has aphrodisiac properties.
- Is he making it all up or is he really going to Bruges?
- There's no trip.
- But he strings her on?
- Yes. The anticipation of a trip, even a fictional one, excites him but, equally importantly, it should keep Esther writing to him.
- How will he get out of it?
- Cancel it nearer the time.
- She must be used to that.

- And after writing to Esther, he answers a message he received some time earlier from the Chiswick woman, the woman he would see later. Remember? The posh one?
- Yes.
- As it's been so long since he first contacted her, he's forgotten what she looks like. He checks her out on her website to remind himself. A red head with large breasts, a bit dumpy. He gets up, locks the door of the office and unzips his fly but then decides against masturbating. Better to write to her and suggest a date.
- His undoing. Chiswick will undo him. Yes?
- That's right.
- Poor Richard.
- Stupid Richard.

❧

- I feel sorry for Richard.
- You always do.
- Do you see him as an addict?
- Well—
- What would his therapist say?
- It all depends on how you look at it. First, it's the person-not-called-Bob who mentions the idea when he presents Richard with the facts. We can sack you for using the work computer to contact those women, he says, but if we say that you're an addict, that you're ill, and you agree to be treated, the situation would be different. Richard is furious. He isn't an addict and is not going to accept that. I'm trying to help, not-Bob says. This is the only way out I can think of. Of course, when the child pornography

III

issue comes up—

- Child pornography? Is that new?
- I might have forgotten to mention it. Anyway, Richard argues and tries to resist all the pressure from the university until not-Bob is told by the VC that Richard accessed child porn sites.
- Did he? Are you sure you want to go there? He can't be that stupid.
- You're not saying poor Richard this time.
- I don't like this.
- He only looks for a few seconds.
- But why have him do that? He isn't a pervert.
- He moves from one porn site to another, accidentally clicks on—
- Accidentally?
- As soon as he realises, he's horrified and moves on but the record remains. So, once that comes out, not-Bob has no means or wish to help him. Richard's desperate to make sure that not-Bob believes him; not-Bob tells him that it doesn't matter what he believes. The computer technicians have a record of him accessing the site and that's that. Richard has no option but to resign.
- Wouldn't they prosecute him? Report it to the police.
- They were going to. However, as not-Bob tells him later, the record disappears. Either they are incompetent in the computer support department or Richard has a friend there. Somebody sympathetic. Perhaps even somebody with similar interests.
- Or, the university tries to keep quiet about it.
- Possible. Certainly, there's no follow up.
- Phew.

- Exactly. Anyway, as for addiction, Anna's the next person who comes up with the idea that Richard's an addict. A few weeks after the revelation, she starts reading about men visiting prostitutes and convinces herself that Richard is ill. In fact, that's her way, one of her ways, of coping. If he's ill, she should stay with him, she reasons. It's as if he had a failed kidney. That's why she insists on his treatment, on therapy. When she explains that to Richard, he dismisses the idea. If there's one thing I can't stand, he says, it is all these bloody amateur psychologists. First not-Bob and now you. Anna isn't prepared to budge, either therapy or they part, she insists. You remember that?
- She isn't a woman to compromise.
- Would you expect her to in the circumstances?
- Possibly.
- Only a male reader would.
- I'm a male reader.
- Even a male reader should have sympathy for her position.
- I do but I think she's too hard on him.
- Talking of addiction, in one of the sessions with Stuart, Richard admits that while he was seeing prostitutes, from time to time he wondered whether he was an addict. So it's not only not-Bob and Anna who think of it. Richard tells Stuart he regularly felt a compulsion to go back to the women.
- Wasn't that because each experience was unsatisfactory?
- One way of looking at it.
- You said that he had persuaded himself that he needed just one more opportunity for a fulfilling experience. Did that make him an addict?
- Well, as you say, he persuaded himself. But wouldn't an

intelligent man understand that he was deluding himself? Anyway, what would he consider a fulfilling experience?
- I don't know. You're the author.
- I don't believe there can be such a thing with a prostitute.
- Why not? I bet lots of men enjoy it.
- How can you say that?
- What do you mean?
- What's your evidence?
- They go back.
- Richard went back and claims he didn't enjoy it.
- He must have enjoyed it a bit.
- So, he's lying.
- Well, I imagine he enjoyed it up to a point.
- I think what he really craves is warmth, more than anything sexual. As time passes, he begins to worry and checks online articles on addiction. He learns that addicts show compulsive behaviour that impinges on other areas of their lives. He manages to persuade himself that he isn't an addict: he has never missed an appointment, professional or social—
- You made him late for Anna's party.
- True. He didn't intend to; he got lost on the way home.
- I see.
- As for addiction, the way he reasons is that he hasn't sacrificed other areas of his life: the family hasn't been deprived of anything and his research is going better than anyone else's in the department. Besides, he's proud that he treated the women with respect, always paid what they asked for; always put the money in an envelope. He believed that a real addict wouldn't have done that.
- What? Put the money in an envelope.

- No, silly. He wouldn't have been so considerate.
- Why not? I thought you said he was doing it for himself.
- Yes. What I'm trying to show is that Richard tries to reason with himself, tries to persuade himself that he isn't an addict because he's in control.
- Right.
- However, he's aware that most of his emotional energy goes into justifying himself and feeding his activity. Sometimes he tells himself that he could have stopped whenever he wanted but in his heart of hearts, he may not believe that. And so he asks Stuart for his opinion.
- What does Stuart say?
- Stuart likes the theory of an American psychologist called Stanton Peele.
- Which says?
- That we're all addicts.
- That's handy.
- Peele believes that our convenience-oriented culture, with its sophisticated technology, our need to seek constant entertainment, escapism, our culture of high stress, our culture that leads us to deny our limitations, seek instant gratification, breeds addicts.
- I could have told you that.
- He says we're all addicted to one thing or another. But some addictions are more obvious than others, some more acceptable than others.
- Exactly.
- He says that you can't only treat the individual, you have to address society.
- Where does that leave Richard?
- To plod on with Stuart. Don't worry; he's having a good

time. He likes Stuart and he feels he has someone to talk to, ask for advice; confide in.

- Anna's addicted too.
- We all are. And you're right: her obsession with prostitutes is a problem.
- She must be spending lots of time on the internet.
- Not only that.
- ?
- I've got to go out now. I'll tell you later.

⚜

- So, how's Anna addicted?
- Whenever she and Richard have sex, the only way she can get excited is by pretending that she's one of his prostitutes.
- She can't be the first woman to have that fantasy.
- Perhaps not but it's different in her circumstances. It bothers her, it makes her feel guilty. She hates the women—
- And yet she's using them.
- Not directly, not by buying them as Richard did.
- Okay. It's not the same but in her mind she should feel uncomfortable.
- She does.
- So Anna and Richard carry on having sex after the revelation?
- Yes. At first, she's disgusted, physically disgusted with him and can't imagine physical contact. At the same time, she knows that if they're to stay together, they should have a sex life.
- I can see that.
- Sarah tells her not to rush into anything. Give it time.

Allow your hurt to heal, she says, but Anna isn't the most patient of people; she doesn't wait.

- You surprise me . . .
- Are you being sarcastic?
- Who? Me? No!
- ?
- Sorry. Tell me. What happens?
- After the revelation, Anna spends two weeks at Sarah's—
- Didn't know that.
- Yes, something like that. Haven't worked it out as yet. She walks out the morning after the revelation and wanders around in a daze, ends up at Sarah's. Anyway, a week after returning home, one evening, after Richard has gone to bed – he sleeps in his study, leaving the marital bed to Anna – she swallows several sleeping pills and drinks a full glass of whisky, almost in one go. She knocks on the door of Richard's study and asks him if he would like to make love. He's startled. Months later he would tell her that at that moment he was afraid of her; he thought she might want to hurt him.
- Understandable.
- What? Her wanting to hurt him?
- No. Him being afraid of her. She's a mad woman. She could bobbit him.
- Don't be silly.
- I wouldn't have trusted her. Mad.
- He made her mad.
- Depends on the point of view. She should have taken control of her responses.
- You've told me all this before.
- But you keep ignoring it.

- What do you want me to do?
- Change her. Make her less nasty.
- She isn't nasty and anyway, this is my novel.
- What's the point of asking for my feedback if you don't take any notice? You never take any notice of anything I say. That's why I understand Richard.
- What do you mean you understand him?
- I can see why he behaves—
- Why he goes to prostitutes?
- He needs an outlet for his frustrations.
- Do you need an outlet?
- What do you mean?
- Answer me. Do you need an outlet?
- This isn't about me.
- You started it.
- It's this bloody novel. I'm fed up with—
- Forget it; I don't need your feedback.

❧

- ?
- ?

❧

- ?
- ?

❧

- Why aren't you talking to me?

- You aren't talking to me.
- I had nothing to say.
- I had nothing to say either.

- Please, let's not escalate.
- Okay.
- I'm sorry.
- I'm sorry too.
- I do like to hear about your novel.
- Okay.
- Please, tell me.
- Tell you what?
- What happens?
- When?
- That time when Anna goes to his room. She's had a glass of whisky and sleeping pills.
- He's afraid of what she might do to him but goes along with what she wants.
- Poor Richard.
- He deserves what he gets.
- I never understand the notion of deserving this or that. Things happen; we do something good or bad and there're consequences but as to whether we deserve something or not, the idea doesn't make sense to me. After all, so much that happens to us is arbitrary. The universe makes no sense.
- I didn't mean to provoke a philosophical homily. It was his action, the choices he made and kept making for a long time, which have brought about the pain for both

him and Anna.

- She's not an easy person to deal with.
- Here we go again.
- Sorry.
- He has no excuse. It annoys me, and I can see how it annoys Anna, when she is seen as a mitigating circumstance. A controlling wife and a controlling mother. What else could poor Richard do but visit prostitutes?
- You tend to accuse me of not seeing Anna's point of view. You don't seem to be able to put yourself in his shoes. At least as a reader, I'm allowed to do that, be sympathetic to one character, but you as a novelist—
- I can see his side of the argument. But that's not the point.
- It never is when it concerns you. Why do different rules apply to you?
- Even if one thinks that Anna is difficult to live with, that doesn't excuse Richard. He is intelligent and he has free will; it's Richard who decides to visit prostitutes and goes on doing it for eight years. And who knows how long he would have carried on had he not been discovered? He has no excuse. Neither Anna nor his mother. Nothing. He wasn't drugged.
- I've looked at some of the stuff you've been reading for your research.
- Yes?
- I came across a therapist who argues that some men labelled sex addicts are actually strong and they have incredible will power. The men are actually self-medicating, that is, dealing with a difficult situation in their lives. While morally Richard has no excuse, I can see why he behaves as he does.

- As long as you don't blame Anna to get him off the hook.
- Absolutely not. Only having a bit of sympathy for Richard. It's like saying: you are guilty but I'm sorry for you.

&

- I miss Tanya. Where has she been?
- In prison, for six years.
- What for?
- Murder.
- A punter?
- No, I don't think so but leave it for now. Still thinking about it.

&

- What happens to Anna's and Richard's sex life after a week of her drugging herself?
- She becomes a prostitute.
- What?
- She becomes a prostitute and Richard is her client. Her only client.
- Is this some silly fantasy?
- You might call it that. It helps Anna. They enact it for three or four weeks.
- ?
- The rules are that he texts her, as if he were a punter. They make arrangements and then she turns up at his home.
- At their home, you mean.
- Yes, but they pretend it's his. A few times they go to a hotel.

- Do you mean they engage in role-playing?
- Yes. And he pays her; don't worry, it's always the same envelope with the same money.
- Don't they get bored with the game?
- They vary it. Anna has acquired wigs, incredibly high fuck-me shoes that she can't imagine ever using for anything else, and a selection of sexy underwear.
- How does Richard feel about it?
- He plays along.
- He has no choice.
- That's what he thinks.
- But that's right.
- Probably.
- Is he enjoying it?
- He has orgasms.
- Daily?
- Yes.
- Quite something at his age.
- He's only mid-fifties.
- Exactly.
- One day, fifteen minutes into the session, after they've shared a glass of wine and gone upstairs, she whips off her wig. I can't do it any more, she says. We sound so false. Nothing I, or you say, excites me anymore. Everything sounds absurd. Shallow.
- That's after how many sessions?
- Twenty odd, or so, three or four weeks, almost every day.
- They seem to have a lot of time on their hands.
- They're trying to repair their marriage. It takes time.
- What does Richard say?
- He apologizes. He thought Anna liked the game. I did

until today, she says. She thinks they should fuck without playing the roles but doesn't say it. She isn't sure whether she's ready for that.

- What a mess.
- She tells him that she can go on for his sake. Oh, no, I don't need to, I was only doing it for you, he says. She stares at him; she doesn't like what she's heard. Does it mean he didn't desire her but was only complying with her wishes? She feels rejected again.
- But what else could he have done? She can't have it both ways. Force him to have sex with her and then complain when he says that he was doing it because he was asked to.
- She realises that herself. But Richard could have been more sensitive; he could have said he was enjoying it. He could at least pretend that he desired her.
- She wants to control his mind, not just his body.
- That's too harsh. You're as insensitive as Richard.
- He's being honest. Points for that.
- No points for insensitive honesty. Sometimes a little lie is helpful.
- I disagree. Besides, he may have desired her but that desire gets overruled by her imposing the game.
- He should make an effort to make her feel better, feel wanted.
- Perhaps he does want her but he might be bad at expressing it.
- The same thing.
- He can't win.
- It's not about winning. If you put yourself in Anna's shoes, you would see she feels cheated. She thought they had good sex and now it all seems pretence.

- But it was a game.
- Only the roles. Not the sex. That was meant to have been real.
- If they both enjoyed it, let alone if they had orgasms, then it was real. I don't see why she complains.
- She doesn't. She doesn't say anything but she's disappointed. Well, okay, the game did turn her on and helped her have sex with Richard, overcome her disgust with touching his flesh, but she also went through the whole thing because she had imagined it would bring them back together. Kick start their sex life.
- Doesn't it?
- Not sure. Have to think about it.

⁂

- Good day?
- No.
- No? Why not?
- Looked over what I've done. What's the point of anyone reading about two people dealing with difficulties in their marriage?
- We've talked about this before. People learn how to behave from stories.
- Maybe, but I don't want to be writing those sort of stories. Didactic, instructive.
- They don't have to be. You wouldn't call *Madame Bovary* didactic or instructive.
- I'm not writing a nineteenth-century novel.
- No, but the reader still gets pleasure from knowing what happens. The reader enjoys seeing people overcome

adversity.
- I don't find it pleasurable.
- Why are you writing this story then?
- The topic interests me but I wish I could do something else with it.
- Like what?
- Not sure what but not a conventional story of adversity overcome.
- You mean they aren't going to get through it?
- I don't know. What happens at the end doesn't interest me in the least.
- That's why everyone reads. You must be the only one who doesn't care what happens in the end.
- I do, but only in terms of structure, not in terms of what happens to the characters.
- What else could you do with this story?
- Perhaps I should write a play. I had this image of an old couple, both in their eighties sitting in chairs, side by side, upstage centre, talking about their lives. In a fairly stylized, repetitive fashion. They never look at each other, simply stare ahead. Each time they start with one of them asking the other whether he or she wanted a cup of tea and then the other would say, remember when you did this and so on, the person would retell an event, all associated with the man visiting prostitutes some forty years earlier, and with the woman coping with the knowledge. At the end of each short scene, the question about the tea would be repeated and the person offering to make it would say: I'll go and put the kettle on. Neither would move. Lights would stay on throughout but there would be a minute of silence between the short scenes.

- Beckett.
- Possibly.
- I prefer your novel.
- What interests me is the idea of obsession. In their old age, the two have lost everything else but their obsession. What happened has taken over their lives and that's the only thing they remember, the only thing they can talk about.
- Desperately sad. I hope that doesn't happen to Richard and Anna.
- You want them to live happily ever after?
- I do. It's warming when you see people stay together.
- A male reader and a romantic, that's what you are.

-
- Tell me about Tanya.
- I can't.
- Why not?
- Because I can't see the point of the whole story.
- I want to know what happened to her.
- She's in prison.
- Still?
- She got six years.
- You're not writing *Tristam Shandy*. You can deal with six years in one line, or no line at all. I don't expect lines that need six years of reading.
- No.
- Let's see. She's in for murder.
- Yes.
- Who did she kill? A punter or that boyfriend?

- Dave.
- Her boyfriend, the pimp?
- Yes.
- Well done.
- Don't ask more. I don't know anything else.

- Good day?
- I don't know.
- ?
- I wrote something.
- Tell me. What happened?
- I can't. It can't be summarised.
- Read it to me then.
- It's not the writing for reading aloud.
- Let me read it then.
- No.
- Please.
- You won't like it.
- Try me.
- Really unsure of what I'm doing.
- You know it helps to read it out.
- Okay. Actually, no. I need to look at it again before I can show you.
- Please.
- Oh, I don't know.
- It might help to get my feedback.
- Okay. Tanya's mind after she has been arrested.
- Thank you.
- It's longish.

- I'll make myself comfortable. *On-y-va?*
- *It was her time now. She was safe. She could leave. No one would stop her. She would be safe. She would not have to see him again. She knew all of that. The voice kept repeating the same thing. But something else, not a voice, a force inside her wouldn't let go. That force made her fetch a knife from a drawer in the kitchen. That force made her walk back to the room. That force made her push the blade into Dave, lying sprawled on the floor, snoring. As the steel went into his chest, he jumped, startled, uttered a cry, of shock or anger – she couldn't tell. Fear ripped his eyes open. He lurched to one side, shaking, trying to grab her, mad with pain. But he was drunk with beer and sleep and she was quicker. In a second, she stabbed him again. Then she stabbed Marvin, mother's old friend, and saw his kind, lined face grimace with pain. And again. And again she had it for Dave. Quick, sharp stabs. In out, faster and faster, like someone going mad chopping onions. Each time she shoved home the knife, his blood spurted its red warmth onto her face, onto her half-naked body, onto the walls around them. It dripped on the carpet; she could feel its drying stickiness on the skin between her toes. Her hand moved as if someone was directing it, pushing it with a long stick like she was a puppet. And the hand carried on working for a long time after he had stopped making any sound. All she heard was the swish as the knife passed through his chest. When she stopped, she was gasping for breath. The swish continued. His body lay next to her like a huge wet sponge. The hard work was over. She could relax. She fell back into an armchair, her legs stretched out. She had no energy left, her body was limp, a rag doll. If he rose now, she couldn't fight back. She was certain of that.*

But he was more dead than the corpses she had seen on the telly. She closed her eyes. She was safe. It was her time now.

She must have dozed off. When she woke up, the blood on her skin had dried. There was daylight and the sun hurt her eyes. Her body shivered with cold. She screamed when she saw him: his eyes bulging like in a horror film. She rushed out of the room. Could he still be alive?

She should wash her hands, her body, the carpet, the walls. And him? If he were dead, she could take him somewhere, somewhere where she would never see him. Hide him. But she wouldn't do any of that. She had killed him. She was going to jail. She grabbed her coat and ran onto the street.

And then she saw him, a big body stumbling towards her. His eyes were bleeding sockets, and he couldn't see his way. But his face was kind, the face of Marvin, smiling, putting out his hand towards her, checking that her body was warm. But the hands were cold, his fingers cold and bony. She ran, her bare feet on the chill of the tarmac. He was coming after her. Slowly. She ran and ran. Then she couldn't see him anymore. But she knew he would come and she was scared.

She banged on the door of a house. She banged and called until a window opened in a room upstairs. And another one in the neighbouring house. Then a door opened and she rushed in. The rest happened to someone else. She watched it from the side without feeling a thing. The people in the house, the police, the ride in the car, the station, the questions – she couldn't tell what they had to do with her – but *the questions, so many questions and the doctor who came to examine her for wounds, the samples of blood they took and the shower. She sat on the cracked tiled floor and let the water run over her head, over her hunched body. She saw herself jumping away from Dave as he pulled off her bra and threw it to Nige. She crossed her arms to cover her naked breasts. Nige sniffed her bra. The other man was laughing loudly and banging his fist on his knee. Come on, give us a bit of fun, Dave said, a bit more, the last bit. He tugged at her knickers. Nige had his hand in his trousers and the other man had unzipped himself and was rubbing his cock. Dave pushed her onto the sofa between the two men and then Nige pulled her on top of him. Gavin was next to him. She felt them pull her knickers off. She hit, and kicked, and scratched. It was this or nothing. She howled and bit whoever she could. Nige was swearing, mad with pain and anger: Fucking bitch, you'll pay for this. She screamed as he hit her on her face and breasts and forced himself inside her. The other man was holding her legs apart. She went on screaming and scratching and eventually the two men left her alone. Can't you shut the bitch up? Gavin shouted to Dave. You need to learn to control your missus, Nige said. The water turned cold but she sat there letting it run over her bare back until someone came and put a towel over her.*

*They told her he was dead and she neither believed nor disbelieved them. It didn't matter. But she was sure she had died. Because everything was different and she was different. She had to be dead. When she was alive, she would feel that force taking over her and then there were things she loved and things she hated, but now it was all the same. She couldn't feel a thing. The next day she was in the holding cell when a man came to see her and said he was her lawyer. He was there to help her and he talked and talked. And that same question that the police had asked.*

*When she had returned from the refuge Dave had been nice, had bought stuff from Iceland and they had tea like a proper couple. And he didn't mind when she wanted to see EastEnders. He made fun of the story and laughed as he talked about the fucking-hell-of-a-cleavage of one of the women but that was all right. And then one evening, as she had taken stuff from under the grill, there was a knock on the door and it was Gavin. He had broken down not far from their place and he wanted Dave to help him. She had offered to go with them – she was happy to miss EastEnders – but Dave said she should stay and watch the telly. So she did. He said he wouldn't be long. But he was. She was already asleep when he returned. She remembered him drunk, lying on top of her, pushing himself into her.*

Sorry, I hadn't realised I'd gone on so much. Difficult to know where to stop. So, what do you think?

- Hang on! That's not your writing.
- Err . . . How can you tell?
- Gosh, it's obvious. Not your style.
- I know but I wish it were mine. I just need something like that here.
- Maybe but . . . anyway, where's it from?
- A short story I came across.
- Really? Why by?

131

- Oh, I don't know. Some foreign woman. Some V Main.
- Never heard of her.
- Me neither.
- But listen, I think it works.
- I know.
- Please carry on.
- Are you sure?
- Absolutely.

- *But why didn't you leave? He didn't listen. Did he want her to repeat it? The evenings after that followed the same pattern: Dave went out, usually with Gavin and came back drunk. Sometimes, when he was on an afternoon shift, Gavin came over with cans of beer and they would drink before lunch. After Dave had turned up for work drunk for the second time, they sacked him. Of course they did; he was a driver for an off-licence. They were strict about such things. Then he started complaining about her not working. She had tried hard, in shops and bars, but there was nothing or else the money was shit – it was better to be on the dole – and every day they argued and he hit her. He said she should go back on the street but she didn't want to do that again. Once they quarrelled and the neighbours called the police but all they did was to tell them to quieten down. That same evening he beat her up so badly that she lost consciousness.*

-

*The lawyer interrupted again with that same question: Why didn't you leave him?*

*She thought for a long time but couldn't think what to say. He was her man, it was proper, it wasn't like Marvin giving money to her mother, it was real, they had dated for real. She wanted to stick with Dave. She could see it wasn't easy for him with no money and no job. She had to help him out. That's what couples did. And he was sorry when he hit her. Sometimes he said so.*

*Tits, give us the tits, come on; that was Nige's voice. And then Gavin echoing him: Tits, tits. She saw herself moving towards the door. But as she turned around, Dave was standing next to her. He took her in his arms and started to dance. It was nice. The men laughed and clapped. Then Dave kissed her and, for a moment, she thought he was thanking her and she would be free to go. She relaxed and let him turn her around, but he surprised her by unclasping her bra. Nige and the other man shouted: Yes, tits, get her here.*

*But you could have walked out? You chose not to, the lawyer said.*

*It was early afternoon when he came home with Gavin and Nige, carrying six packs. Dave pushed her into the bedroom and closed the door: Look, help me out. Nige has promised me a job. He spoke quietly, as if not wanting the others to hear. A proper job, quite a few things actually. She didn't believe him. He said: Nige's brother-in-law is opening a bar and needs a bouncer and someone to fix things, be around. He's doing me a favour, so I want to keep him sweet. She asked what he wanted her to do. A slow dance, and strip a bit . . . put them in good mood . . . that's all. She stared at him. Three men drinking together and her stripping. That won't be all. She didn't do that anymore.*

*Look, Tan, you don't want to work.*

*I do. I'll get something. They promised me, she said.*

*Oh, they promised you, he mocked. And you believed them? He turned away from her, lit a cigarette. Have you forgotten Lilla? he shouted. If I had a job, you could look after her; she could be here. I'm doing it for both of us. He sat on the bed, smoking. She looked out of the window. The back yard was paved; that's where they kept the bins and Dave's broken motorbike. She remembered the day he tried to repair it and couldn't and made it worse. That was the time when she was cheated and taken to that house. She had agreed to do a job in the car and then there were three men and they had raped her. And they didn't even pay and then Dave had hit her when she got home and had no money to give him. But it was the motorbike he was really angry about. She forgave him for that.*

*The question again, that question she had come to dread. He was thick, this lawyer.*

*Tan, come here, babe, he patted the bed next to him. She didn't trust him, but she obeyed. Come on, sit down. He put his arm around her, kissed her on the cheek and whispered into her ear. It's all right, if you don't want to help. But . . . I need work . . . and it's fucking hard to get anything. Nige has promised. I could start next week. That's why I got the beer . . . to celebrate. He ran the back of his hand across her cheek. You get my drift? He kissed her on the cheek.*

*Stripping only, no more?*

*Yeah, of course.*

*Only the shirt and skirt off. I can keep the bra and knickers on, yeah?*

*Yeah, whatever.* He stood up. She wanted to help him but she wasn't going further. She'd do the dance and nothing else. Dave walked out. Through the closed door, she heard him talking to his friends and them laughing loudly.

*Stripping for three drunk men? In your home? That's mad. You were asking for it.* This lawyer was doing her head in. Why was he so stupid? It was a little strip, nothing else. Helping out.

A few minutes later, one of them shouted: *Show! When's the show starting?* She heard clapping and cheering. She thought of calling Dave to tell him she was afraid they wanted more than a strip. Then she heard him: *Come on Tan babe, we're waiting.*

She opened the door and walked in. Dave had already moved the coffee table to the side and she stepped onto the rug in the middle of the room. Nige and Gavin were slumped on the sofa, beer cans in their hands. Dave sat in the armchair. The stereo was playing. She got on with it straightaway, thinking that the sooner she started, the sooner it would be over. It was important to please Dave by pleasing the men, but she was wary of getting them excited. They leered at her and she hated that. It would be all over soon. She made herself think it was somebody else stripping, not her. Her mind was on that Great Yarmouth promenade, breeze in her hair, the ice cream van playing a jingle. She unbuttoned her shirt slowly, but made sure that her eyes did not meet the men's. With each button she unfastened, the men cheered. Then she took off her shoes, one by one, and the tights – she had no time to put on stockings – caressing her legs, as if trying to memorize their shape. She moved around, wriggling her hips, dancing barefoot in her skirt and bra. Nige tried to touch her but she managed to move away and he mumbled 'teasing bitch'. She went on dancing, but the other man shouted 'skirt off, skirt off' and she began to tug at the zip, pulling it down and then a little bit up until it was done. She took off the skirt as slowly as she could and then carried on dancing. That was that. No more.

But even then you could have walked out. What was he saying?

Gavin pulled her knickers off and forced himself inside her, Nige doing the same from the back. She fought them, biting and scratching, that force inside her giving her strength, incredible strength. And then them shouting shut the bitch up, but running out, running away from her.

This story's no good. You consented. Why didn't you leave? The lawyer asked. Best to ignore him.

Dave was furious, strode towards her but she was quicker.

*She locked herself in the bathroom. And then it was quiet. She couldn't remember how it happened but soon he was asleep. No, she is sure he wasn't dead. She heard him breathing, his chest rising.*

*And then? Did he wake up and attack you with a knife and you had to defend yourself? The lawyer said.*

*No, she was sure that he didn't. He wouldn't have done that. He was a fist man, not a knife man. Besides, he was too drunk and when he fell it was like he had passed out. In a second he was fast asleep. But she was very angry with him. Mad at him. That mad like when you think I could kill that person. I could chop them up into tiny bits. But when she went to fetch the knife she wasn't thinking that. She wasn't thinking anything. She was doing things. No, that's not true. Her body was moving, without her doing anything. Her hand grabbed the knife and pushed it inside his chest and out. She couldn't stop the hand.*

*And then the lawyer said that what she had said didn't make sense and that she was in trouble if she stuck to the story. He said that it didn't happen like that. He said he knew what had happened and that she should listen to what he said. He was going to write it down and she would sign it and then say the same thing to the police. Why was he asking her then? She said it loudly but he didn't answer. Instead, he repeated that she had killed her violent boyfriend in self-defence. He wrote that down in his notebook. But was it Dave or was it Marvin with his kind, lined face who was dead, she wondered. The lawyer stared at her before repeating that it was Dave who had fetched the knife from a kitchen drawer and who had tried to stab her but she had fought him and killed him in self-defence. It was self-defence, she had to remember that. She didn't care either way. She had told him what it was like – she knew, she watched it happen – but if he wanted to believe something else, it was none of her business. She was fine. That force had let go of her.*

- She's really captured here.
- You think so?
- Yes, Tanya comes off. She really does. Poor woman.
- Of course, as I read it to you, I changed the name. It's something else in the original.
- The psychology works; you can feel what goes through the mind of a poor abused woman. A woman traumatised over a long time and now in shock.
- I agree.
- So, what are you going to do? How can you use it? I mean this other writer's story?
- I don't know. Maybe I should try to get in touch with her.
- She is no name. She ought to be pleased if you give her exposure. Free publicity.
- Perhaps.

⁂

- How was your day?
- Okay. Yours?
- Nothing to report. Things don't happen to me. They happen to you.
- Only because I make them up. Isn't it strange that I find

Richard much easier to write than Anna?

- Because you steal from me.
- An occasional, non-defining detail here and there.
- That's an understatement. Your problem with Anna is that you think she's wonderful, perfect and bears no responsibility for what happened. Whereas, in fact, she's a control freak—
- I'm tired of you being so obviously male.
- I'm an honest reader. Your first reader; if I don't tell you, who will?
- Tell me then.
- Anna's story is too simple. She thinks her marriage is wonderful, faultless and when cracks appear—
- Cracks? You call that a crack? It's a huge abyss. The ground under her feet disappears.
- A matter of perspective. With her, everything's wonderful and then everything's awful. Always white or black. Life's mostly grey. But Anna can't see that. Another thing you have in common.
- Thanks.
- You both tend to exaggerate, over-dramatize.
- Not difficult when your husband goes on visiting prostitutes for eight years.
- ?

※

- How was your day?
- Fine. Yours?
- Fine.

- How was your day?
- Nothing much to report.
- Are you not speaking to me?
- You never tell me about your day.
- Because nothing ever happens.
- To me neither.
- But you have this interesting couple with you. I keep thinking about them.
- ?
- I'm convinced Richard wasn't after sex.
- Tell that to Anna.
- She must know.
- Even if she could believe that, it wouldn't help her.
- Look, it's a real tribute to the author if a reader, albeit the husband of the author, thinks that Richard wasn't interested in sex.
- How do you work that out?
- I'm trying to say that you manage to communicate the complexity of the situation. It's not as simple as most people would think: a man has no sexual partner and so he goes to a prostitute. You explode that myth.
- ?
- I'm paying you a compliment.
- Thanks.
- I mean it.
- Okay then.
- I just wish Anna could be a bit more rational and accept that Richard wasn't after sex.
- Why?

- It would help her deal with the situation. She would realise that Richard's activities had nothing to do with her.
- Oh, since when do you think so? You've been blaming her all along.
- Well, she has a lot to answer for: she isn't easy to live with. That would have contributed to Richard's feelings about himself. But she isn't responsible. Another man would have coped differently.
- Glad to hear that.
- Another man might have murdered her.
- Don't be ridiculous.
- The way you have presented it, we can see that with Richard there was fertile ground with his mother, the way he was brought up.
- Blame women. Blame mothers.
- Again, a tribute to you that you've created this background for Richard. It makes sense.
- Not sure I want that. It's much more complex than what you call the fertile ground created by his mother and wife.
- It's also worth remembering that it took Richard many years before he did anything. A cumulative effect of Anna's control over him.
- Don't be silly.
- Well, it's good the way you have done it. People will feel sorry for him.
- I don't want people to feel sorry for Richard.
- Why not?
- That's not the kind of novel I had in mind.
- This may be better.
- It's not the kind of novel I like. It's not my novel.
- If you don't want people to feel sorry for Richard, don't

make Anna so unpleasant.

✦

- Good day?
- Not bad. And yours?
- Busy. Bob has some new ideas on how to increase our applications. I'm supposed to think of how to attract more Asians to history. He's bonkers: he compares our figures to Law and Dentistry. We can't compete with them. We aren't too bad on women though. You know what Bob said? Proudly, without any awareness of the language he was using: Birds have always been flocking to us. Nancy and Moira rolled their eyes but no one bothered to tell him.
- What a great sentence. I need it.
- No, don't. It's not yours.
- What do you mean it's not mine? It's not yours either.
- It's stealing, it's plagiarism.
- Don't be silly. Words are in the public domain.
- My colleagues would recognise it.
- Bob's not the first person to have said it.
- Please don't.
- I've got to. Imagine the situation: Bob, or Rob, as he will be in the novel, is lecturing Richard on sexism, or rather on what a female colleague has pointed out to him to be the unacceptable politics of Richard's activities and then he says something like that. Beautiful irony. I can't let it pass.
- Think of something else.
- Not as good as this.
- Don't you always say that you can't stand novels that

imitate life?
- Just a little borrowing here and there.

⁂

- Good day?
- Yes. Fine, thank you. And yours?
- Fine, thank you.
- You won't tell me?
- Nothing to tell.
- Who was it today?
- Richard.
- What's he been up to?
- Not much. Sitting at home.
- Has he stopped working?
- Yes. They had a deal: if he resigns, nothing will be on record.
- Not sure that would be allowed. Not with that paedophile site visit -
- Well, as you know, they lose, or some sympathetic soul gets rid of, the evidence for the visit to the child porn site.
- Oh, yes. But he used computers at work to arrange prostitutes.
- Yes, but - anyway, Bob promises—
- Rob.
- Yes, sorry. Rob or not-Bob promises that there will be nothing on record. Perhaps he's wrong and can't give that assurance. But that's what's said.
- So, Richard sits at home and does what? Research?
- No. He's too low to think about it. He sees Stuart once and sometimes twice a week and that's all. Most of the

time he's on his own.

- Where's Anna?
- Busy with the Gallery and with her own life.
- She hasn't left him, has she?
- No, but she's rarely at home.
- Can't be good for Richard to be alone like that. Who knows what he might do.
- Stuart tries to encourage him to get involved in something to occupy his mind.
- Hope he doesn't take up golf.
- Don't worry. Richard's not the type.
- You mean because I'm not.
- Nothing to do with you.
- If you say so.
- Richard dismisses all the suggestions Stuart makes. Then he comes across a site for single parents, registers under an assumed name, takes on the role of a man in his thirties, a widower, with a two-year old daughter. In no time at all, he has several single mums writing to him.
- Oh, no.
- In fact, nothing happens. He enjoys making up stories about his life, giving advice on pushchairs, playgroups and so on. It amuses him how he can find all the information on the Internet and pass it on to the women as his experience. With one of the women, he establishes regular contact. She wants them to meet, sends pictures of herself and her daughter and so on. Richard always has an excuse, either Imogen - his fictional daughter - is ill or his dead wife's parents are coming to stay, or he's travelling and so on. He's aware that after a few weeks he becomes dependent on the contact, obsessively checking his messages.

- So, the therapy hasn't worked.
- What do you mean?
- Well, isn't this virtual relationship rather like what he was doing before?
- Less dangerous.
- He should have other resources. Stuart should have provided him with something.
- I agree. Lots of therapy's useless.
- That was your experience. Many people would disagree.
- Perhaps.
- So, the single mum?
- They talk on Skype but he's careful to make it known that his old machine has no camera. Sometimes it crosses his mind that the woman might get dependent on him, might be hurt. At the same time, he tells himself that one day he will stop the contact – he's been careful and the woman would have no means of tracing him – and as for the guilt, well, he can't be responsible for her.
- More fool her to believe what people tell you in a chat room.
- Besides, he reasons, he hasn't been completely useless; he has given her some valuable advice.
- What a desperate man he is. Lonely.
- You could say that.
- Does he tell Stuart about this?
- No. He's aware Stuart wouldn't approve. He convinces himself that Stuart encouraged him to meet people and engage in something that would occupy his mind.
- Poor old Richard deluding himself as before.
- Yes.
- Are you leading us towards an unhappy ending?

- What's an unhappy ending?
- Will he succumb? Will he go back to the prostitutes and that will be that? Anna will leave him.
- I don't know.
- You haven't decided as yet?
- No. All options are still to be considered.
- That's a relief.

❧

- Dying to know. Who was it today?
- Anna.
- Good. Missed her.
- I thought you didn't like her.
- The woman I love to hate. But I've been wondering what's happened to her. How is she coping?
- She walked out on Rachel, the therapist, you remember that?
- Yes.
- She feels she can help herself.
- In what way?
- Well, two things: to find answers as to why Richard needed prostitutes—
- But there's no answer. I thought that much is clear.
- Yes, and she's beginning to accept that she'll never understand. But there's something else too. You remember that she feels rejected as a woman.
- That's what she keeps saying.
- She has affairs. She thinks of it as a way of coping with being rejected
- How does she find the men?

- Ads.
- Oh yes, I remember. The builder and the bald lawyer, the one pontificating about wine. Is that all?
- There are a few others.
- At the same time?
- More or less. She starts seeing one of them, Patrick, regularly. In fact, she usually spends Thursday nights at his flat in the Docklands.
- What does Richard say about that?
- Nothing. He feels he has no right to complain. In fact, Anna tells him that she's staying at Sarah's. He chooses to believe her; he doesn't want to know.
- And then one day, Anna will realise how all these affairs are meaningless and that none of the men is as good as Richard.
- I doubt it.
- So you know what will happen?
- No.

꩜

- Good day?
- Not bad. Yours?
- Nothing to report.
- Okay. I understand.
- Who was it today?
- Richard.
- What's he been up to?
- He's in New York.
- Looking for a job?
- He has one.

- Already?
- He contacted a prof he knows – they've met at conferences many times – a guy who in the past has tried to tempt him. Richard might have been interested but Anna wasn't keen on leaving London. This time, he flies over and within days bags the job.
- At last something good happens to him!

※

- How was your day?
- Not as good as I'd have liked. And yours?
- Nothing unusual. Who was it today?
- Richard with Stuart.
- You mean he's back in therapy.
- Oh no, I'm redrafting an earlier chapter.
- What happens?
- Richard talks about Anna, about her vulnerability.
- ?
- I'm showing Richard at a therapy session, one of the later ones. The reader is told that the sessions have drifted into topics not directly related to the main issue and Stuart lets Richard talk about whatever he wants. After all, Stuart believes that what Richard really needs is a friend, a shoulder to cry on. So they talk about cricket – a subject Anna finds unbearably boring and she makes Richard feel guilty when he checks the results—
- Sounds familiar.
- I'm not the only woman who can't stand sport.
- As long as he isn't me.
- Or the other way around.

- ?
- ?
- What do you mean?
- Nothing.
- Why did you say it then?
- A joke. Don't be so touchy.
- Well—
- Do you want to know what happens?
- Yes.
- Sure?
- Yes, I do.
- Well, Richard and Stuart talk about music and Richard enjoys that. He complains that Anna has a very narrow taste—
- You just don't want to give her anything that isn't you.
- A little detail of characterization here and there.
- I wish you would make things up, not take them from us—
- From me.
- Not quite. It may be about you but what Richard says, those are my words, my words in Richard's mouth.
- No one will know.
- Sometimes I think you're writing this novel to expose our private life—
- That doesn't make any sense. You aren't doing what Richard is doing.
- How do you know?
- ?

※

- Why did you put that inscription above your desk?

- What inscription?
- That quotation.
- Which one?
- You know which one.
- I don't. I have lots of notes pinned above the computer.
- You know very well what I mean.
- ?
- As if it's not enough for everyone to recognise us.
- ?
- You need to rub it in.
- ?
- Stop raising your eyebrows.
- I don't know what you're talking about.
- You do.
- No. I don't. I have loads of notes, sayings, quotations.
- I am talking of the one about sadness one can bear if put in a story—
- Oh, that.
- Yes, oh, that.
- Isak Dinesen. A good sentence for a motto, don't you think?
-

- ?
- ?

- Good day?
- Fine. Yours?

- Nothing to report. How's the writing?
- I don't want to talk about it.
- ?
- I said I don't want to talk about it.
- Why?
- Because it doesn't feel right.
- The writing or talking about it?
- Neither.
- Can I help?
- No.

※

- Good day?
- Fine. And yours?
- Nothing to report. How's the writing?
- Nothing to report.
- ?
- ?

※

- ?
- ?

※

- How was your day?
- Good. Yours?
- Okay. The same as always. Who was it today?
- Richard.

- I may be wrong but you seem to have more on Richard than on Anna.
- There's more to come on her.
- I think you find him easier to write than her.
- Do I?
- You said it once.
- I don't think so.
- You take things from me and make them Richard's but you're more circumspect with your own past.
- That's unfair.
- That's what it looks like to me. Remember, I'm your reader, the first and most critical.
- Biased too.
- I disagree. I strive to provide honest feedback.
- Sometimes you do.
- So, what happened to Richard today?
- He admits to Stuart that he wasn't telling the truth. Not completely.
- What about?
- His earliest sexual experience.
- Masturbation and the stained pyjamas?
- No, the first time he had sex, or tried to.
- Yes?
- Well, he tells Stuart about a prostitute, a prostitute he went to see after the two failed attempts to have sex with that girl from his school. He was too ashamed to try again with the girl and so he got some money together, money from his paper round - and visited a place where he had heard street walkers operated. He had to make a couple of trips before he had enough courage to speak to one—
- But—

- Sorry, can I finish?
- But I—
- Let me finish. Her name's Paula and she's only a couple of years older than him. He finds her kind and she talks to him and doesn't rush him and so he manages to control his orgasm. A week later he goes to seek her again but she isn't there. He goes again and again but can never find her. Another woman talks to him but he doesn't go with her. He even fantasises of going out with Paula, helping her leave prostitution.
- This is ridiculous.
- Why?
- I don't see why you need it. It's perfectly okay for him to have that girl in an abandoned house. Why a prostitute?
- Because of his later interest in prostitutes. He has had a good experience and he wants to repeat it. He is searching for Paula in all the other women.
- Bullshit.
- Look, from what I've read, most men who have been with a prostitute once, revisit that experience.
- Why haven't you told me this before?
- Haven't I?
- No, you haven't. Don't pretend.
- It might have slipped my mind. In any case, I haven't told you everything that's in the novel. Just enough to whet your appetite so that you buy—
- It's not funny. As for this Paula, I draw a line here.
- What do you mean?
- You can't have that.
- Why not?
- You know very well why.

- No I don't.
- Listen, you take it out or . . .
- Or what?
- Please. Take it out.
- Why?
- You've gone too far this time.
- Don't walk away. I don't understand why you mind so much.

❧

- Hello.
- Hello. How was work?
- Nothing to report.
- You still haven't told me why you mind that Richard—
- I don't want to talk about it.
- Why?
- Don't push me. I've had enough of Richard.
- ?
- I'm not like him and I'm fed up you stealing my life and giving it to him.
- ?
- She wasn't called Paula.
- ?
- She wasn't called Paula.
- What? You don't mean—
- Yes.
- I had no idea.
- I don't believe you.
- It's a experience for a working class boy and, I suppose, not just for working class but many young—

- I was only seventeen. And drunk.

⁂

- Good day?
- Yes. Yours?
- Fine, thank you.
- I've gone back to Richard talking to Stuart about Anna.
- Yes?
- He tells Stuart how he used to think of Anna as very strong but recently he's realised how vulnerable she can be, just like him. He says, it's as if before she could cover it up, but she can't anymore. In the past, he says, the only issue Anna appeared to be vulnerable about was her ageing, her fear of the menopause and that used to irritate him—
- Not again.
- What?
- Do you do it to annoy me?
- You may not believe it but it's not about me and it's not you. Loads of women fear the menopause and loads of men don't understand and it's useful for the story—
- You say that about everything.
- I really need this one. I don't see why it bothers you if I take stuff from myself.
- Because it always involves me.
- No one would know. You're too sensitive. As for Richard, he admits he wasn't much help to Anna. He couldn't bear her complaining about the lines on her face or worrying about her periods stopping. Just a natural, biological process he would say but Anna hated that. As if natural meant anything. An academic should know that, she would

155

snap. I could see how my response irritated her, Richard says. But what else did she expect me to say, he asks.

- I'm with him on that one.
- Surprise, surprise.
- So, what happens?
- He didn't think of her as being vulnerable. He thinks she was making a scene, drawing attention to herself. But when he told her about his secret life, he was shocked to see how she reacted, what it seemed to do to her – that's when he saw her as truly vulnerable.
- Because she didn't shout?
- Perhaps.
- He should be thankful for small mercies.
- Don't be insensitive.
- Well, I'd be glad if your reactions didn't include shouting.
- I would be glad if you didn't provoke me to shout.
- When do I do that?
- Do you want to talk about us or what happens in the chapter?
- Not sure.
- Okay then.
- Look, I'm sorry. Don't go away. Please. Tell me, what happens next?
- You aren't interested.
- I'm. I really am. Look, I'm sorry.
- Richard says that was the first time he saw her as defenceless, fragile. Anna completely withdrew into herself, became somebody else. He thought she looked mad and yet she was completely still, quiet. Instead of exploding, she imploded, he says. She scared him. He thought she had gone mad, in that really frightening, quiet way. It crossed

his mind that she might have lost the power of speech, like that woman in the Carter novel.

- Which one?
- That's the question Stuart asks and Richard at first can't remember the title of Angela Carter's novel but after a moment it comes to him: *The Magic Toyshop*.
- Oh, yes. Does Stuart know it?
- No, I don't think so.
- Whether she shouts or goes silent, her reactions seem completely over the top. No wonder Richard is scared of her. She makes up for the silence later, anyway.
- As usual, you're being unfair.
- I'm a reader. Remember? It's up to me to have my own interpretation.
- A very biased one.
- That's what you think.
- As for Richard, he says he knew she wanted to humiliate him but he wasn't in a position to refuse anything.
- He should have put his foot down.
- Well, he didn't. He's more caring than you.
- Bloody hell. You use every opportunity to put me down.
- Who's shouting now?
- Just showing you what it's like.
- What's like what?
- Being shouted at.
- You've shown me that before.
- Not as often as you have.
- You're more irritating. You provoke me more than I could ever provoke you.
- That's not true. You don't know yourself.
- Look, I don't want to argue.

- Don't you?
- No, I don't. But you do.
- I don't.
- Well, let's not argue then. And let's leave us out of the story.
- Okay.
- Do you want me to tell you what happens next?
- Yes, all right.
- Richard says he cannot see how he could have gone through with it.
- But he agreed to?
- He had no choice.
- Poor Richard. And when she is back with him, she presents him with the ultimatum that he should have counselling. No compromise. That's horrible. I understand how he feels.
- What do you mean? That I put conditions and—
- I'm talking about Anna, a character in your novel.
- I see.
- Well, sometimes you do behave like that.
- So, I was right. You think I impose conditions.
- Sometimes. But look, I don't want to talk about us.
- Fine.
- What else does Richard say?
- Well, now it's him who's playing the amateur psychologist. It's bizarre, he says, that Anna's been reading about sexual addiction and claims she can identify all the signs in me. But the irony is that she's become an addict herself. And she can't see it.
- Good on you, Richard. Spot on.
- This isn't a football match. No cheering.
- Okay, tell me what happens in the second half?

- Ha, ha. Well, Richard talks about Anna's obsession with checking prostitutes on the Internet. For six months she was on their sites every day. He couldn't understand what she was looking for. She rang a few, and e-mailed one of them, pretending to be him. She wrote to the woman that his wife had found out about his activities and the prostitute wrote back, advising him to work on his marriage. Richard is astounded that the prostitute wasn't bothered about her loss of business.
- The whore with a golden heart. Sometimes clichés come alive—
- You won't believe it.
- What?
- That's exactly what Richard tells Stuart.
- What?
- That sometimes clichés come alive.
- You've been stealing from me to make him and now it's the other way around. I'm copying him.
- Don't say that!
- It's not my fault if I'm turning into Richard.
- What you do is your responsibility.

- Hello.
- Hello.
- Good day.
- Yes, thank you. Yours?
- Yes, thank you.

- Hello.
- Hello.
- Good day?
- Yes, thank you. Yours?
- Yes, thank you.

❦

- Do you think Richard has a good heart?
- What do you mean?
- I was thinking about him talking to Stuart about Anna's vulnerability.
- Yes?
- Why is he doing it? Is it because he cares about Anna?
- Up to the reader to decide. It could be that he's trying to absolve himself of any responsibility.
- Responsibility for what?
- For her state of mind. For her obsession.
- ?
- Well, as he talks, he tries to explain, he tries to make sense of what's going on. He's talking to Stuart but he's doing it for himself too. You could also say that he's trying to assuage his guilt.
- He can't be responsible for the way she reacts.
- He provokes her reaction.
- You could say she provokes his behaviour, his interest in escorts.
- Rubbish. Anyway, it's more than an interest.
- We will never agree on this one.
- You're so entrenched in the stereotypical male position.

- I wonder if your readers will be split according to gender.
- I don't know.
- What else happens in that chapter with Stuart?
- Richard talks about how painful he finds it to see Anna so ill with her obsession. And it's not just him; Sarah's noticed the same thing, he says. He finds it painful when she compares herself to the women he met, poring over their bodies, assessing them, wondering why they were more appealing to him than she was.
- But they weren't. It should be clear to everyone that it was more complex than that.
- True, but that's a rational explanation. You can't expect a woman in Anna's position to think like that.
- Maybe not immediately, but after a while, she should make the effort.
- How long is a while?
- A week, a month. I don't know.
- Richard says that Sarah tried to talk to Anna about female solidarity but Anna blew up. What bloody female solidarity did they have in mind when they slept with my husband? That's what she asked. Richard says he loves Anna and it hurts him to see her destroying herself. She isn't herself. She's hardly done any work in the Gallery; she doesn't even seem to care about art anymore.

⁂

- How was your day?
- A sentence came to me. I heard Anna say: I didn't know he knew how to lie.
- By he you mean Richard?

161

- Yes.
- Who does she say it to?
- I'm not sure. That's the problem. But I would like her to say it. It's a simple sentence. A sad sentence. A poignant sentence. I think it expresses much better her pain, her distress, her sadness, her sense of betrayal than all that about her being rejected as a woman.

※

- Good day?
- No. Not at all.
- ?
- Done nothing. And you?
- Fine, it was fine. What's the problem?
- I don't know where I'm going.
- You always say that.
- That's different. That's when I have lots of ideas and they all fight for attention but now, now I feel I have nothing more to say.
- Perhaps you've reached the end of the road.
- ?
- Richard has a job in New York and you have to decide what Anna does. I hope she joins him—
- And they will live happily ever after.
- It's up to the reader to think that or not. I wouldn't expect you to spell it out.
- Good to have a happy ending.
- You know I don't like such stories.
- What, happiness?
- I don't like narrative closure: boy gets his girl, the character

grows up, the mystery's uncovered, the murderer discovered. How tedious.
- Not at all. Perfectly satisfying.
- Absolutely not.

⁂

- Good day?
- So so. Not much writing done. Mostly thinking.
- What about?
- What to do with Tanya.
- Oh, the young prostitute. Well, she comes out and she finds a nice bloke.
- Don't be silly.
- Why not?
- She's had enough of men.
- She finds a nice woman.
- No.
- Then what?
- She finds herself.
- She finds herself? How?
- That's what I'm thinking about. I know: Tanya gets cancer.
- A completely arbitrary decision. Why would you have that? What would that mean? Poor Tanya.
- There's no meaning to getting cancer.
- I didn't say that. I meant in the narrative.
- Okay. Something else happens: a pimp, a pimp whose women no longer want to work for him is angry at losing his source of income and kills her.
- She might just as well die from a meteorite falling on her on a London street.

- That would convey the absurdity, the meaninglessness of death. But that doesn't fit in this kind of novel.
- Absolutely not.
- Okay, then. I'll leave Tanya be.
- Thank God for that.

※

- Good day?
- Yes. Yours?
- The same as always. I'm all ears.
- Anna has had a successful day negotiating collaboration between galleries all across the country. She feels on top of the world. It's a Thursday, a day when she normally sees Patrick, one of her men.
- How many has she got on the go?
- Four.
- Four?!
- Well, Patrick is the serious one; she meets him at least once a week. The other three, once a month or so; with them it's all fairly casual.
- But not with Patrick?
- Yes and no. They've both made it clear from the very beginning that they were having an affair and nothing more but recently he suggested she should move in with him. He has a Docklands flat, one of those minimalist, loft affairs.
- Exactly the kind of thing Anna likes.
- Yes, she does, but so do many people—
- Nothing wrong if she has this in common with you.
- True.
- There're few surprises with Anna.

- There will be for other readers.
- So, what happens?
- Well, Anna tells Patrick weeks in advance that she won't be able to see him or stay the night on that particular Thursday. At first he doesn't mind; they are planning to meet on Friday instead. But when she speaks to him on the phone in the morning, he sounds unhappy. She rings him at midday again and he says he's looking forward to an early night as he's getting a cold.
- And will need someone to nurse him—
- What do you mean?
- Only joking.
- He adds she shouldn't worry about not meeting. When her event, at which she pulls off an excellent deal for the Gallery, finishes earlier than expected, and she's feeling on top of the world, she wonders whether she should ring him and they could still have their usual Thursday evening. She deliberates for a while, wondering whether to go to his place - she remembers that he wanted an early night - or to join her friends at the event for a dinner. The latter is attractive as she's on a high and feels she needs to be with people.
- People who admire and adore her.
- Yes. What's wrong with that?
- Synchronised sycophancy. She's so insecure.
- We all are.
- And then?
- She vacillates, eventually deciding against the dinner with friends as one of the people there has been after her.
- I thought she would have liked that. Good for her self-confidence, part of her affirmation. Isn't that what she's been

seeking after what happened?
- Yes, but not from anyone.
- What's wrong with this guy?
- Not sure. He's boring and he loves the Pre-Raphaelites. She can't be interested in a man who likes Rossetti, that fool Rossetti, she says.
- Nothing to do with you and your taste in art.
- Of course not. It's Anna, Anna, the gallery owner. No one who loves art can take seriously those Victorian illustrators.
- Okay. So, she goes to see Patrick and as she comes unannounced, there's a surprise for her. He's just been screwing—
- Is it so predictable?
- It doesn't matter if it's predictable. Remember you aren't writing a novel where you surprise the reader with plot devices. Other things carry off your writing.
- Are you being ironic?
- Not at all.
- Well, what you say isn't true of this novel.
- Maybe not. But it works. And so it's all over with Patrick and she realises how wonderful Richard is.
- Something like that.
- A happy ending. Hooray!

∗

- Good day?
- Possibly. Have another idea for Tanya.
- I hope she's saved.
- Yes, she saves herself by saving others. She runs a charity, something called Futures—

- It'll be all right once they get together. It's only pre-meeting anxiety.
- Yes, on Tanya's part. Anna, however, doesn't know where Sarah's taking her.
- Why not? Why doesn't she tell her?
- Well, Sarah's fed up with Anna's hatred of prostitutes and she thinks that meeting Tanya, recalling the memories of their student days and campaigning to help sex workers might shift Anna. She thinks if she were to tell her, Anna wouldn't go.
- Deception. Anna won't be happy about that.
- As for Tanya, she can't do any work all morning. She remembers how her brain used to freeze. Now she tells herself that she will have to guard against that, stand up for herself.
- How old is she now?
- Forty-nine, a few years younger than the other two.
- How big is the charity?
- Oh, I don't know. I suppose, let's say, it's a small organisation, eight women and Tanya.
- But she's used to dealing with people in public life?
- Oh yes. Let's say she's twice been to 10 Downing Street; she's been invited to talk to ministers; she's organised fund-raising galas; she's met celebrities. She has her professional role and people respect her. But before they arrive, she keeps thinking how those two could turn her back into a twenty year-old street-walker, lost for words, doing what they want her to do.
- And do they?
- Wait a minute.
- Unable to work, Tanya has been drawing. We see her

contemplating two new pastels, one of the daffodils in a vase on the table and another of the blue hyacinths growing in a pot on the window ledge.

- She draws? Is that new?
- Don't be so impatient. She's looking at the drawings and it crosses her mind that they could be presents for her visitors. She smiles at the thought. No, she wouldn't give the drawings to them. They might say how lovely they were and she couldn't bear to be patronised. They'll see all the stuff hanging around – they could hardly miss the dozens of frames covering the office walls – but she won't admit that they are hers. She knows she's improved after more than twenty years. Lots of people liked them, which was useful in prison where she could exchange them for favours, a haircut or a manicure. Even the guards would grant her privileges in exchange for a drawing or two. And outsiders too, people who come to discuss the charity, journalists have praised them too.
- Tanya the artist. Lovely.
- She isn't an artist. The pictures were her midwife, helping her give birth to a different Tanya. They are small, drawn on sheets from an A4 sketchbook and they don't take long to complete, even though she works slowly, her mind on each detail. She understands the process: drawing takes her out of herself, or of the self she doesn't want to be. When she traces the outline of a petal, she is there, on the leaves, her mind seeing nothing but the flower. And when she comes back, she is clear-headed and she can do whatever she needs to do. Tanya remembers how throughout the trial she sat in constant numbness. The prosecution claimed she had shown no remorse. But the fact was she

felt completely dissociated from the person who had killed Dave and even from the person on trial. It was only after she was sentenced to life imprisonment, and when she was left alone in a cell, that she woke up. Then the real anger kicked in. She was ferocious, livid, attacking her solicitor and her welfare officer. They put her on medication for two years. Chemical imprisonment.

- This is all from her point of view?
- Oh yes, Tanya's the focaliser here.
- And Anna and Richard are the other two focalisers elsewhere?
- Yes. As for Tanya, in the second year, she made friends with two women, one of them a prostitute, and it was while talking with them that she realised how her whole life had been one of abuse, first by her mother and her mother's lovers and then by Dave and the punters.
- That's good. A real step forward.
- Yes. But a long time passed before she agreed to counselling. Then she was angry with the therapist, losing her rag in every session. One day the therapist came in with a sketchpad, pencils and a flower pot. As soon as Tanya started screaming, she stopped the session and they both drew the flowers. That helped beyond belief. Soon she was drawing whenever she felt anger raising its head, which was pretty much most days.
- Is that a technique a therapist would use?
- I came across it somewhere. Anyway, on the day the women are coming, Tanya remembers how in the morning she dressed more formally than she would for an ordinary day at the office, because this isn't an ordinary day. Her past is coming back into her life and she mustn't let it take over

her present. Besides, she has to show those ex-students that she's no longer the pathetic whore who needs their help, a young woman, bruised by her boyfriend, turning up at their consciousness-raising group. She's the Director of *Futures* and that's why they are coming to see her. She considered putting on her new M&S grey flannel dress, or the red Wallis skirt that makes her feel elegant, but in the end she opted for a dark trouser suit and high heels – her confidence outfit.

- So, the reader gets inside her head here, as she is waiting for the other two to turn up.
- Yes.
- The idea being that you communicate her anxiety and feed in some background, that is, what's happened since the prison.
- Exactly. You speak like a writer, the kind of writer that sells.
- Don't tease me. Have you got more thoughts from her head?
- Yes. Tanya contemplates her looks: her short hair is completely grey these days, but that's fine. She's noticed that most people show more respect to older women. In front of her visitors she will keep her glasses on all the time – even though she's short-sighted and anything near will be out of focus. She has been on courses; she knows how important it is to project the right image.
- They are meeting on her territory: a clear advantage.
- Something like that.
- So how does the meeting go?
- Sarah keeps asking questions, while Anna listens quietly. Tanya catches the two women exchanging glances. Why

are they here? She remembers that Sarah said something about Anna needing to meet her. Sarah asks about prison and how *Futures* started and she doesn't mind telling them, but why, Tanya wonders. Why does she want to hear it? She must know it from the article. She must know the facts, what the journalists called facts. But not all the facts.

- That's what's going on through Tanya's head?
- Yes and she thinks how no one knows that it was the first time in her life that she had felt safe. Safe in prison. Like never before. But she doesn't tell them that. Nor does she ask any questions. But Sarah talks about their lives anyway, a woman she used to live with, my partner Jocelyn—
- Oh, yes, we've met her.
- No we haven't. She's dead when the novel opens, dead for four years.
- Okay, not in person but we've heard of her.
- Good of you to remember.
- You don't credit me but I'm a careful reader. I remember that Jocelyn died of breast cancer.
- Yes. Then Sarah mentions Anna's daughters and asks Tanya about her own daughter. Tanya wonders whether she should tell them. She could be thirty or so, Sarah says, smiling, asks Tanya if she is a grandmother. Tanya says: Lilla was adopted. It was for the best at the time. We aren't in touch. That's the truth, she thinks. But the whole truth is that at the time she couldn't have cared less what happened; if anything, she was relieved that she didn't have Lilla to worry about. Before that there were all those years of anger, anger about having to be a mother, wanting her daughter out of her life so that Dave wouldn't complain. Tanya thinks how she sent her daughter to her mother,

knowing that with granny, Lilla might be subjected to the same kind of exploitation that she herself had suffered at the hands of those old men. But she didn't care about that. Somehow she even wished it on her, that's how angry she was. And now the whole truth is that whenever a prostitute in her early thirties comes to *Futures*, Tanya hopes, she hopes to God, that it's not her daughter. She stares at the young women, assessing their facial features, their figures, their hair, thinking whether anything reminds her of Lilla. Perhaps that's what drives her: her delayed maternal instinct. She's working to save those women from themselves, helping them find new lives, as if they're all her daughters. She tells them it's not too late; it's never too late, it wasn't too late for her. And they don't often believe her but at least some of them try.

- Arthur Miller, *All My Sons*.
- Thank you.
- Well, Tanya's really found herself. She now has a mission in life.
- Isn't it all a bit too neat?
- I don't think so. It makes me feel good when such things happen.
- Does Sarah tell her what they came for?
- No, it doesn't seem appropriate. Anna looks too hostile, too closed in.
- Tanya gives them leaflets: *Prostitutes Speak Out* and *What Can be Done?* Anna doesn't look at them. Instead, she turns towards Tanya and says: The women aren't the only victims. The men's lives and those of their families, they can be destroyed. Their marriages never recover and you can't imagine what it's like when—

- Does she tell her what's happened to her?
- No. She stops herself. Her voice is trembling and she is angry. Sarah puts her hand on Anna's arm, as if to comfort her.
- Wouldn't Anna be sympathetic to the idea of criminalising the men?
- Yes, but it passes her by. All she's thinking of is her own situation.
- There's a novelty.
- Don't be so judgmental. Try to understand why she is like that.
- Tanya must have noticed that something is bothering Anna and that she wanted to say it but then didn't.
- Yes, Tanya did notice but she is aware of her next commitment and so she agrees that men and their families are victims too and her tone makes it clear she doesn't want to discuss it there and then.
- Good. Confident Tanya.
- Do you think this is a plausible transformation?
- It must happen sometimes.
- I hope so. Anyway, before they leave. Sarah invites Tanya to visit their gallery. She says: Now that we know what you do, perhaps we could work on something together. A project. We could use art as therapy, helping the women, don't you think?
- Marvellous. Love this.

- Good day?
- Not really. Yours?

- Nothing to say. What's wrong?
- I'm stuck. I feel I haven't done justice to Anna.
- In what way?
- She's had this terrible shock, she's terribly hurt, humiliated even. I was thinking how her friends, the ones who know what happened and, you see, she's the sort of person who would have told quite a few people—
- Well, that's her fault.
- She did it when she was in shock and needed support. And later she worries that some of them might assume that she wasn't interested in sex and that therefore poor Richard had to go elsewhere.
- Anna strikes me as the kind of person who wouldn't bother very much with what other people think.
- Usually not, but she doesn't like others to think that she's cold or prudish. Because that's what people think when they hear that a man in a relationship is looking for sex elsewhere, particularly with a prostitute.
- But you know that's not the case. Anna knows that's not the case.
- But others don't know it. I didn't know it before I read up on the issue.
- I don't see that's her main problem.
- No, not the main problem but she does think about it and it bothers her.
- Typical of Anna to see everything from her own point of view.
- What do you mean?
- Well, having told all those people, she doesn't worry what they think of Richard—
- He's the guilty party. What she told others is true. But at

the time it didn't cross her mind what they might conclude about her.

- Come on. It's not that simple.
- What I'm saying is that this terrible thing happened to her and she's trying her best to sort it out—
- That's hardly her best.
- Look, she could have just walked out on him.
- Might have been better for both of them if she had.
- Is that what you think? I can still do that.
- Is this a threat?
- What do you mean? How can I threaten you by making a character do something?
- Okay then. Let them be.
- ?
- Look, I misunderstood. I'm sorry.
- Okay.

꩜

- Good day?
- I don't know. Yours?
- Fine, thanks.
- So, what happened?
- Still trying to work out the ending. I was wondering what would happen if Richard were to turn down the job offer?
- Why would he do that?
- To stay with Anna. She doesn't want to move to New York.
- Because she's with Patrick.
- Not anymore.
- So, what's he going to do?

- Richard?
- Yes, if he doesn't go to New York? What else is there for him?
- I can work out something.
- And if he's bored at home—
- Mmm.
- He visits a website and contacts a woman and so on. All over again. A relapse.
- Exactly. What do you think of that?
- Poor Richard. I want him saved. I want him to pull himself together. He could ring Stuart, get help.
- He doesn't.
- Anna's bound to find out.
- I can leave that for the reader to work out.

- Good day?
- Not really.
- ?
- Got nowhere. Moving in circles.
- Sometimes you need to do that. As you know.
- I do. But it's so dissatisfying.
- It'll be better tomorrow.
- You're just saying it.
- You have to believe it.
- I'm not a believer, not a natural believer.
- It's bound to be better.
- It could be worse. It could always be worse.
- Yes, but eventually the trend changes direction.
- Eventually.

- Don't be so pessimistic. I told you, you made too much of Anna's reaction. What a drama queen!
- Only a man would say that.
- Doesn't Sarah tell her to pull herself together?
- Yes, but not that she's making too much of it. As for me, it gets me down seeing them move in circles.
- It's her fault.
- What do you mean?
- He wants resolution. He wants to move on. She doesn't; she wants to dwell on the past. She wants to make him grovel.
- She doesn't want to. She can't help it.
- She can seek support.
- It didn't work.
- She didn't try hard enough. Screwing half a dozen men won't help.
- Poor Anna.

❧

- You seem happier today. Tell me. Who was it?
- Anna.
- What has she done?
- Remember Patrick coming to the door in his dressing gown and her realising what he has been up to? So, he runs after her, barefoot down the stairs but she tells him that he doesn't owe her an explanation. He remonstrates with her downstairs at the entrance to the block but she doesn't want to hear him. She goes home. She checks her messages and writes back to all the men she's been seeing.
- You mean the other three?

- You remember the number. And a couple of others. Maybe.
- Quite something. What I don't understand is why she's upset about Patrick if she's been seeing others as well?
- It's the deception that hurts. She didn't hide it from him. She felt she had the right to her own life and her own freedom. He said it was okay with him but that he didn't want that kind of freedom for himself.
- Doesn't seem to be fair. One rule for him, another for her. Typical of Anna.
- That's his choice.
- I know but still—
- You could look at it as his way of making her feel guilty for not being monogamous like him, his way of making her abandon everyone for him. A kind of passive pressure. Very cunning and very dishonest.
- But it didn't work.
- No. Anna enjoys seeing others too; she can't see why she should give them up. None of the men, and the same is true for Patrick, have everything she's looking for in a man. But together, they are great; they complement each other.
- Is that your fantasy? You used to say something similar: every man is inadequate so you have to have several and mix and match their best points.
- Not a bad idea, you have to admit.
- What is it I lack?
- How long have you got?
- Thank you.
- Look, we have to stop this.
- Stop what?
- Turning the discussion to us when we are talking about the novel.

- All right. My question: had Patrick given Anna advance notice of the change of rules, that is, of him being as free as she was, would she had been okay with him having someone else around?
- Probably.
- Probably?
- She would have to be. Of course, the announcement would make her consider what has changed in their relationship for him to take the step.
- Knowing Anna, that would make her insecure.
- Possibly.
- So Patrick can't win.
- It's not about winning. Why do men always talk about winning?
- He has no way out.
- Out of what?
- What he really wants is for her to give up the others.
- But she doesn't and so he takes the same right for himself without telling her.
- He was alone and he invited this woman and without thinking he went to bed with her. He didn't do anything wrong since she's seeing three other men; besides, she's married—
- What about deception?
- That's a minor point under the circumstances.
- A minor point? If you think so, it's obvious why you can't understand Anna's reaction to what Richard has done. It's the deception that hurts more than anything else.

❧

- How was your day?
- Fine. And yours?
- Not much to say. The same as usual. Tell me, has Anna given up all her men?
- Yes. After leaving Patrick, she wrote to each of them, saying that she could no longer carry on meeting them. Next, we see her alone at home – Richard is visiting a school friend – and she goes to the garden; it's a mild spring night and she sits on a bench, sipping a glass of white wine. It's been a long time since she felt so content.
- A year or two?
- Two years more likely. She sits outside, it's eleven o'clock and she hears a blackbird sing and she thinks how unusual it is for the bird, this sole bird singing beautifully, to be around this late at night. She decides that the bird's singing for her. She listens for a while and all she wishes is that Richard were with her, sharing her delight. She goes in and rings him. He's in a pub with that friend and she speaks to both of them. She tells Richard that she misses him and she's looking forward to seeing him. I'll be back tomorrow, he says.
- He comes back and that's the end of the story.
- Not sure.
- What do you mean? They've suffered more than enough. They deserve a good ending.
- Okay.
- Hooray.

☙

- All done?

- More or less.
- You should be pleased. I am.
- I'm not sure about that ending.
- No, don't say it. It's great.
- It's too neat. Too pat. All hunky-dory. Not my kind of thing at all.
- Now you're the old cynic.
- It's too much like wishful thinking. Candy-floss.
- Perfectly plausible. People go through difficult situations and survive, face problems and overcome them. Anna and Richard are two intelligent, articulate, experienced people; I really can't see that they shouldn't be able to work it out.
- But they are also emotional people, dealing with a highly emotional issue.
- Richard isn't emotional.
- You think not?
- That's my impression.
- Not sure.
- Anyway, they can't throw away twenty-five years of marriage.
- If there's no other way—
- But there always is. Remember Anna listening to that blackbird and wishing that Richard could share the joy with her. If she thinks like that, she loves him. She will want to save the marriage; she will make the effort.
- Maybe she will.
- And he will and that's all done.
- Well, there are other factors.
- Such as?
- I don't know.
- You mean Patrick or one of the other men.

- Oh, no. That's finished. Maybe one or two get back to her and try to change her mind but it's not worth mentioning.
- Then what else?
- I don't know. Something else could happen that would prevent them from staying together.
- Nothing will happen. They'll be all right. Richard will go to New York and Anna will join him. She could start a gallery in New York.
- All right.
- Nothing like happy ever after.

⚜

- Good day?
- Okay. Yours?
- Fine, thanks. So, working on a few finishing touches?
- More than that.
- What do you mean?
- Been thinking how many things could happen to those two.
- Such as?
- Richard's flight back from New York could crash.
- That's silly. Why would you do that?
- Their story is unlikely to have a happy ending.
- More likely than the plane crashing.
- He could get a terminal illness.
- Poetic justice?
- Perhaps. A happy ending doesn't fit.
- Why?
- He shouldn't be rewarded for his misdemeanours.
- What about her and her misdemeanours?

- You mean her lovers?
- Among other issues.
- Her behaviour is only in response to his.
- You could say the same about his being in response to hers.
- No, you can't.
- I disagree.
- Fine. I still don't want a happy ending. Richard's bound to go back to prostitutes.
- Why do you say that?
- Because he never properly addressed his problem.
- You mean the problem of Anna?
- Don't be ridiculous. She is not a problem. I mean, he never confronted why he saw them.
- He seemed convinced he wouldn't go back.
- People are capable of telling themselves all manner of lies in order not to face the truth.
- Perhaps, but plane crashes, or terminal illnesses are last resorts for writers who don't know how to end a story.
- True: I don't know how to end the story.
- But you have ended it. He has a job in New York, she realises that he's better than the other men she's been seeing and she decides to make an effort with him. He's happy with that. They start a new life. They've both learned from the experience and the future looks positive, full of hope. Readers like that. After all that depression, the reader needs an upbeat ending.
- My writing isn't about what the reader needs or likes.
- What's it about then?
- I'm interested in what the story needs.
- And what's that?
- I don't know. That's what I keep thinking about.

- How will you know?
- It should feel right.

⁂

- How was your day?
- Fine, thanks. Yours?
- Fine, thanks. Any more thoughts on the ending?
- Yes.
- And?
- Something else happens.
- No!
- Well, you remember the circumstances I was talking about? The circumstances beyond their control?
- ?
- Well, the university that offered Richard the chair has found out about his past.
- So what? He had the contract. They can't pull out.
- They can. The contract was conditional on his references.
- Didn't he have an agreement with not-Bob that if he resigned, he would get clear references?
- He did but, as you would know, in case of someone so high up the academic ladder, references don't matter. I don't think they'd have even bothered with that. Richard is too well known in the field.
- So, what's the problem?
- Well, someone somewhere must have talked. Some jealous colleague might have rung Richard's new employer or someone might have been gossiping at a conference, something like that. Word gets around.
- No!

- So, here we go: Richard wakes up slowly, feeling the warmth of the sun shining through the dormer window. He thinks of the night before. He and Anna made love and he wishes she were with him now and he would take her in his arms. He's a lucky man. It's all turned out fine. The only slight cloud is Ursula, his stubborn daughter and she will come around. Too much happiness. How wonderful it feels after everything he's been through. And then he's downstairs leisurely making coffee and reading the paper when the postman rings the doorbell.
- The bringer of dreadful news. Go away the postman!
- It wouldn't change anything.
- Does he ring twice?
- Ha ha. Richard signs for the letter. He looks at the post-mark. Must be some additional contract material, he thinks. He's relaxed as he opens the envelope, takes a sip of coffee before he looks at the letter. It says that after con-tacting his previous employer and taking up his references, they have to withdraw his provisional offer of employment. It ends with: We regret to inform you that you were not successful in the final stage of the appointment process. We wish you well with your future applications and the development of your academic career.
- Bastards.
- Richard stares at the paper in his hands. It is embossed with the University's coat of arms. The heading and the signature look genuine; it's the words that are unreal. And then he has a flashback. Images of his three-day trip to New York flick through his mind. He sees himself saying goodbye to Rosalyn, who would have been his secretary. He remembers her as a petite, black woman, immaculately

turned out; he found her attractive and was looking forward to working with her. For the briefest of moments, he allowed himself to wonder whether she was married.

- Oh no, don't make him think like that.
- Why not?
- Takes away his dignity.
- Isn't that how a man like Richard would think?
- Possibly but—
- But what?
- I don't like it. Are you going to tell the reader how the Yanks found out?
- I leave that open but that's a question Richard asks. He doesn't doubt the references would not have mentioned it.
- Bloody puritans on both sides of the Atlantic. He has a fantastic research record, he's an excellent teacher, but to them all that matters are a few extramarital excursions.
- A few extramarital excursions. Hang on. Let me take it down.
- For God's sake. Now I'm channelling Richard. Or is it the other way around?
- Sorry. You don't mind, do you?
- I do.
- This fits so well with his line of thinking. A few extramarital excursions – such a good phrase. Shows how he plays it down! He still hasn't realised the enormity of his offence.
- Don't judge him because of me. They're my words, not his.
- The same thing.
- Don't say that.
- You're thinking like him. You've become him.
- I'm not him.
- I'm not responsible if you begin to behave as if you were

a character in my novel. Another case of life imitating art.
- You have stolen parts of my life—
- What I've used from you could be from anyone. No one's life is unique.
- You've turned me into him.
- As always, you exaggerate.
- I've had enough of this novel.
- ?
- You've been writing this story to get at me.
- ?
- You aren't going to deny that.
- Don't be silly. Do you want to know what happens next?
- I don't care.

❦

- Hello.
- Hello.

❦

- How are you?
- Fine. And you?
- Fine, thanks.
- ?
- I'm sorry about the other day.
- Okay.
- Look, I do care. Your writing matters to me.
- Okay.
- I like to know what you're working on.
- Good.

- I always want to know what happens next.
- The reader's curiosity.
- Nothing wrong with that.
- No.
- ?
- Anyway, now, Richard is sitting on the sofa, with a letter in his hand, for a split second, he's lulled into a fantasy of travelling back to that time, that time ten years earlier when he had everything and he frittered it away so carelessly. If only, if only he could turn the clock back.
- New York would have been a second chance.
- Yes, but with that gone, he can see that he'll never be able to work again.
- Poor Richard.
- And if he publishes, a reviewer might refer to his past out of spite.
- That's unlikely.
- Maybe but that's what he thinks.
- Okay.
- He stares at the letter in his hand. The words blur; a tear rolls down his cheek and falls on the paper. And then another, and another until the print is completely smudged. He lets go of the letter and buries his face in his hands. His body is shaking. He opens a bottle of whiskey and drinks from it.
- Poor Richard.
- And then he has another flashback. He hears Stuart at one of their early sessions: What we need to work towards is to reconnect you to your sense of self-respect, family and society. How hollow those words sound now. He falls on the floor, curls up and sobs. His body feels weightless.

Slowly, the memory of the letter comes back to him. A dream. A nightmare. The realization hits him, punches a hole in his body. Bloody Yanks don't want him. He doesn't want them either.

- That's right. He should pull himself together. There must be other opportunities. He could do something else. Or write books under a different name. It's not the end. Can you pass that on to him?
- Not up to me to interfere. You know how they say the characters have their own lives? At a certain point they become independent.
- Bullshit. You don't believe that.
- Do you want to know what he does next?
- Tell me.
- He sits up and rubs his face with both hands. He becomes aware of how quiet it is at this time of the day, late morning. Not a sound. As if the world had ended.
- You mean that crosses his mind?
- Yes.
- That's a good end to the novel.
- Don't be facetious.
- Well, it's a silly thought to give him.
- And he thinks, what next? Today, tomorrow, ever? He picks himself up, shuffles to the kitchen and pushes his head under a running tap.
- Yes, yes, pick yourself up. Splash cold water on your face, Richard. You can still make it.
- Back in the lounge, he dials a number, listens to Stuart's recorded message and hangs up. He rings Anna, listens to her recorded message and hangs up. He rings again. Dear Anna, please, please pick it up, he thinks.

- That's bad. When you need them, they're not there. What a bugger. But don't give up. Don't go back Richard, please.
- He grabs a coat and walks out, through the park, towards the Thames. He moves slowly, buffeted by the wind. He stops and watches the river, looks up at the clouds racing across the sky. Virginia Woolf walked into the river, stones in her pockets. Would it have been a slow, painful death? How does one do it? Drugs? Despair? Or both.
- Is that what he thinks?
- Yes.
- Come on, you're not going to let him kill himself.
- Not up to me.
- Don't be silly.
- So, he's in the park and something rubs against his trousers: a dog presses against him and lifts its leg.
- That's good. A comic moment. That should make him smile.
- Well, it doesn't. Being mistaken for a lamppost isn't funny.
- Okay.
- And so he moves away, the dog stands still, confused. A gust of wind rushes through the reeds along the banks. Shivering, he pulls up the collar of his coat and walks away. There isn't a soul in sight. The dog must have been a stray, like him, but it didn't stay. He sits on a bench, surrounded by silence. The sky is covered with heavy clouds. Suddenly it's dark.
- Il pleure dans mon cœur. Comme il pleut sur la ville.
- Exactly. Like you, I imagine, he can quote Verlaine.
- Why do you say that?
- Would Anna be married to a man who can't?
- I suppose not. She's a snob like you.

- Thank you.
- As for Richard—
- I doubt if Verlaine comes to his mind as he sees darkening skies.
- No.
- Penny for his thoughts.
- He's no longer a husband, a lover, a friend, not even a prominent historian. The Centre he gave birth to is old enough and strong enough to survive on its own. He should be proud of it but, like the parent of a child who's left home for good, he's been deprived of purpose. He's no longer Richard Bates, let alone Professor Richard Bates.
- Self-pity.
- I suppose so. You can't expect him to be strong and buoyant at this point.
- I don't like the direction in which those thoughts are taking him. Nor that mention of Woolf.
- Wait and see. His teeth rattle with the cold. He stands up to go, but where? He searches his pockets for a tissue and finds an old, scrunched up travel card. It has a mobile number written on the back and the letter 'E'. Esther: he remembers copying it from a website. He never rang her. The last time he e-mailed her was more than a year ago. Would she still remember him?
- Is that a prostitute?
- Yes, the one he used to write to and even sort of invited to join him in Bruges, and then cancelled. And she's the woman Anna wrote to from Richard's address, pretending to be Richard.
- I see.
- Yes, and, pretending to be Richard, Anna wrote that his

wife had found out about his activities and so he had to stop. Esther advised him to work on his marriage.

- A whore with a golden heart.
- So you said.
- Poor chap. His therapist is unavailable, his wife is unavailable; all he has is a prostitute.
- He walks on, reaches the bridge and turns towards the high street. He enters a pub, orders a double brandy and goes to a table in a corner. The place is crowded, but no one sits next to him. He drinks quickly, keeping his eyes on the table. After a while, he takes out the ticket with Esther's number. His heart is racing as he listens to the ringing tone. No one picks it up. He doesn't mind either way. Nothing matters.
- I like that: nothing matters.
- Why do you like that?
- Because it shows that he doesn't need a prostitute, I mean, for sex: all he needs is a human soul. Someone to talk to.
- He shoves his mobile back into his pocket, walks to the bar and orders another double brandy. Someone takes his seat and he stands at the counter, drinks up and walks to the door.
- Someone could talk to him in the pub. Someone could make a comment about the weather, something like that and he could respond. He could still be saved.
- Outside the pub, a middle-aged Asian man hands him a card. I've got it somewhere. Let me read it out to you.

*Professor Sahib*

*International Renowned Spiritual Healer/Clairvoyant.*

*The only man who can solve all your internal problems
and help with many more problems within a shorter
period of time than anyone else, like the return of your
loved ones, success in marriage with someone you always
loved, losing weight, exams, success in business, impotency/
infertility, court cases, all sorts of black magic, bad luck,
addiction, anti-social behaviour, depression, stress, job
interviews and immigration cases.*

*No more worries, 100% Guaranteed.*

*Your pain is my responsibility.*

- Where did you get that from?
- Emile gave it to me. He collects them. People hand them
  out round where he lives. North London. North East.
- I see. So, does Richard consider giving the professor a call?
- You can't see him doing that.
- Why not? He's a desperate man. He could at least have a
  word with the chap giving out the cards. Professor Sahib
  could save Professor Bates.
- No. Richard tears up the card and throws it onto the road.
- That's not kind.
- His mobile rings. He stares at the number, not recognizing
  it. Hello? Who's that? You rang me, he says. She claims
  that he rang her. Then it dawns on him. Rrr . . . is that
  Esther? Sure man, that's me, she says and again asks who
  he is. It's . . . I'm Alan, Alan Roberts.
- Would she remember him?
- No, not by name. So, she asks again who he is and he

explains that he used to write and mentions the Belgian trip that alas didn't come off.

- And she remembers.
- Yes. She says: Hang on, man. I get it now. Fucking hell. That's you. Your wife wrote to me . . . did you know that, she asks. He apologizes and Esther says she didn't mind but found it a bit strange.
- Hang on. Didn't Anna write to her pretending to be Richard, or whatever he was called?
- Alan Roberts.
- Okay. So how does the prostitute know that it was his wife writing?
- Right. You're right. I forgot that. Unless she came clean to the woman—
- Did she?
- I don't know. Missed that one. Will have to go back. Thanks for pointing it out.
- Continuity. That's why I'm here.
- And then Esther asks him what he wants now. He says he doesn't know. That's no use to her. She's a businesswoman. She tells him to make up his mind and get in touch when he knows what he wants.
- She's the only person he's had a chance to talk to after the shock.
- Yes, and he doesn't want her to leave him now. The thought terrifies him.
- Poor Richard. Whores were his downfall but a whore may be his saviour.
- He says he wants to see her. She's surprised. When he insists, she says she charges more for emergencies. He doesn't mind. He says he's not after sex. She says he'll still

196

have to pay. She asks him where he is. He has ended up in Putney and she gives him the name of a hotel nearby. He waits for her in the lobby, drinking brandy from a small bottle he's picked up at an off licence. She arrives by taxi little more than an hour after their conversation. It's two o'clock in the morning and the lobby is deserted. She's six foot and twenty stone, much larger than he expected from the photos on her website. The man at reception nods at them as they pass.

- He doesn't sound to be in a fit state to be with her.
- No, but as he said, he wasn't after sex. He needs someone to hold him.
- Poor Richard. But he could still be saved. Anna could ring. Wouldn't she be worried that he wasn't at home?
- She's away. Visiting a gallery outside London and attending some dinner.
- Bugger. That's too much. What about Stuart? Wouldn't he ring him back?
- Unlikely. Richard didn't leave a message. As far as Stuart is concerned, Richard is through, what with the job and all the prospects. He would have no reason to think there was anything urgent. A missed call doesn't mean much in the circumstances.
- So, that's it. He's back where he started.
- Wait and see.
- You mean there's hope?
- Judge for yourself. Now, they're inside the room, he gives her five hundred pounds, in crisp notes, withdrawn barely an hour ago from two different accounts; she kisses him on the cheek. He slumps into an armchair. You don't seem very lively. What's up? She asks. When he doesn't answer,

she says: Look, let me show you what I can do. She twirls, holding up the ends of an imaginary skirt. He stares at her, not knowing what he wants. Would you like me to do, say . . . a dance for you? She winks at him. He shakes his head. The room is warm and he's overcome by tiredness; he feels like burying his face in her large body and sleeping. He says: Can you hold me? She stops moving, gives him a quick smile and nods. He doesn't look at her as she undresses. They lie on the bed and she envelops him in her arms. They don't speak and he dozes off. When he wakes, Esther is still lying next to him. He remembers the letter and starts crying. She presses her body against him; he feels her warmth. He wishes he could stay like that forever.

- Poor Richard.
- And then the phone rings.
- You mean the hotel phone?
- No, his.
- Who would call him so early?
- Anna?
- Would she? At four, or five in the morning?
- Okay. What about a fire in the hotel, everyone has to get out—
- Richard on the pavement half-naked, standing next to a prostitute?
- All right. But then, the situation might sober him up . . .
- Perhaps. You could give us a number of different endings. Leave it to the reader to make a choice.
- Do you think so? I don't think publishers like that.
- I didn't think you cared what they like.
- I do with this one. I need to get it out.
- I see.

- Anyway, there's no fire alarm. The next thing he sees is Esther checking her mobile, one arm stretched onto the bedside table. Shit man, I didn't mean to stay the night. It's six already, she says. She sits up and pulls off the cover. Now, he has an erection. Stay. I'll get the money. She stares at him. I promise, look, let me give you my credit cards, my driving licence, my wallet, everything . . . if I don't pay, you keep them. Steady on, man, I don't want your stuff, she says. He's grateful that she doesn't leave the bed. He moves in between her legs, pushes open her thighs and, flanked by mountains of flesh, his mouth starts to work. He wants time to stop; he wants to spend the rest of his life licking her soft labia, burying his head between her thighs. She says: It's wet. Here. Her foot moves across the sheet. Did you? She giggles and pulls him up towards her, kissing him. You naughty boy. Doing it on your own, she teases him.
- He has come?
- Yes.
- Hope it's not his last orgasm.
- You're funny. Anyway, he moves his hand across her body. Her skin is smooth and he wants her to hold him tight, make him secure. She does and after a while, he says: Will you crouch above me, with your back to my face? Sure, honey, she says. She squats above him, the two black globes only millimetres above his face. He goes on licking her. The room disappears; now it's only him and her in the universe. She moans: Ahh, man, you're good, here, yes, that, more here, yes, yes, yeees man.
- Would a prostitute do that? She seems to have forgotten herself.

- That's right. And so she checks herself, moves away from him. But she can't help enjoying it. She laughs. Her arms squeeze him. Again, she remembers and she says: No, stop it. You'll make me come. I don't do that. But he carries on, ignoring her. He has never licked anyone like that. She moves away. He starts crying, pleads with her to come back. He says he needs her, he needs her more than he's ever needed anyone. She asks whether he's all right. She is concerned. He doesn't answer. He lifts his face towards her, sticks out his tongue. She stands up and picks up her handbag, rummages inside. She sighs, checks herself again: Fucking hell, man, why am I doing this? Breaking the rules. She drops the bag and turns towards him, staring hard. Esther, think. Don't, she says to herself. He begs her to come back. She shouts at him to shut up. She retrieves the handbag from the floor, unzips a compartment and takes out a small purse. What the hell, she says, you're so fucking odd. I'll make an exception.
- Would a prostitute do that?
- This one does. She takes out a small capsule and hands it to him. He doesn't know what it is. She smiles and says it's a fun pill. A popper. Makes you love it, man, she says. He stares at her, holding the pill between his thumb and index finger. He thinks of antibiotics. Esther bites into the capsule and sticks it under his nose. Yeah, man. Inhale, she says. A present from Esther. Lift you up like never before. What about you? He asks.
- Kind Richard. Even when he's down he thinks of the other.
- Esther says: Your tongue gets me as high as I can go; no need to waste it on me. She laughs. He stares at her. Trust me; it's okay. You'll love it. Here, take a deep breath. He

inhales. She watches him and changes her mind. She breaks a capsule and sticks it in front of her nose, takes a deep breath. Lovely, let's go, she says. She settles her buttocks above his face and he licks her, pushing his tongue further inside her, rubbing his lips against her labia. She moans, louder and louder; her moans turn into screams. He goes on licking; her body is writhing above him; her buttocks pressing down on his nose and his mouth, squashing him. The lack of air makes him light-headed and his own pleasure increases. He gasps for breath but licks and licks. His cock is about to burst; the sperm could penetrate the wall; his body knots with pain and then every last drop is spent. But he licks and licks and licks . . . hears her screaming, pushing down on his nose and mouth . . . his body presses down . . . his arms flay about in the air, like the feelers of an enormous insect. Each time her buttocks lift up, they crush down with a stronger force. He wants to scream, but has no voice and then there is nothing . . . a mass of flesh flattening him out . . . out . . . on . . . and he is going . . . going . . .

- ?
- ?
- Is this a pastiche of porn writing?
- I wasn't thinking of that.
- I see. But I can't tell what happened.
- What do you mean?
- Is he dead or is that an orgasm?
- Either.
- What did you want it to be?
- I don't know. It's up to the reader.
- No!

- I'm just another reader.
- Don't give me that. You're the author; it's your story.
- Not anymore.
- ?
- It's yours now.
- Okay. If it's mine, then Richard emerges from this shaken but determined to fight. He goes to Stuart, tells him what he's done and Stuart advises him not to say anything to Anna. They start working together. Gradually Richard recovers. He learns to cope with disappointments, with low moments in his life, whether they're personal or professional. He works as an independent researcher and lives off writing books, mostly popular, historical biographies. He and Anna stay together.
- That's a different story.
- That's the story I want for them.
- You old sentimentalist.
- Nothing wrong with that. What's the point of having a depressing ending? You need to give your readers hope.

- How are you?
- Fine. And you?
- Fine, thanks.
- Good.
- I was thinking—
- About what?
- You and Anna.
- Yes?
- She's a copy of you.

- A bit. You said that before.
- More than a bit.
- We share a few things.
- In what ways is she different from you?
- Well . . . I don't know. For example, she runs a gallery, I write.
- Is that all?
- Well, I don't know, can't think of anything else right now.
- I feel you were trying to tell me something.
- Tell you something?
- Yes.
- What do you mean?
- Do I need to spell it out?
- What are you talking about?
- You know what I mean.
- No, I don't.
- Think.
- I'm thinking.
- Think harder.
- I don't understand what you mean.
- Anna has four lovers.
- So?
- How many have you got?
- Don't be ridiculous.
- How many have you got?
- Don't be ridiculous.

- I've been thinking.
- ?

- I've been thinking.
- You've been thinking.
- I've been thinking about your novel.
- And?
- I want you to destroy it.
- What?
- I want you to destroy it.
- You must be joking.
- Look, I'm serious.
- But why?
- You only wrote it to trap me.
- What?
- It's too close to us. Everyone will know what's happened.
- What do you mean?
- Everyone will know.
- Don't be silly. They will see it's fiction.
- No, they will assume it's really happened.

# POST SCRIPTUM

- Hello, darling. Good day?
- Yes, fine. And yours?
- Fine, thanks.
- Nothing happened?
- The usual. Five days to opening but this time it's all in place.
- That's something. Sarah must be pleased.
- We all are.
- Dinner?
- Yes, what shall we make?
- Let's see what's around.
- Oh, before I forget, that editor, Paul something, you know the one you introduced me to at your second book launch . . . ?
- Oh yes, what did he want?
- He wants Alan Roberts—
- He didn't say that?
- Yes. Why not?
- He always calls me Richard and his assistant refers to me as Mr Bates.
- Well, this time he used your nom de plume.
- Are you sure?
- Absolutely. He said he would like Alan Roberts to review a novel.
- What's it about?

- A couple. She's a writer.
- What about him?
- A reader.
- And?
- The novel's about her writing a novel.
- Is that all?
- Apparently, it causes them to split up. Hang on: maybe not. Can't remember what happens at the end.
- Doesn't sound very promising . . .

# ACKNOWLEDGEMENTS

I AM GRATEFUL to the women who shared their stories with me.

Thank you to my daughters, Rebecca and Hannah Partos, for their love and inspiration.

Thank you to my late friend Max Lab for sharing his medical knowledge and comments on the plot.

Thank you to Emil Simpson for Professor Sahib's card.

Thank you to Anthony Rudolf for his insight, generosity and continued friendship.

Thank you to Peter Main, my most first reader, for his help and feedback.

## NEW FICTION FROM SALT

RON BUTLIN
*Billionaires' Banquet* (978-1-78463-100-0)

NEIL CAMPBELL
*Sky Hooks* (978-1-78463-037-9)

SUE GEE
*Trio* (978-1-78463-061-4)

CHRISTINA JAMES
*Rooted in Dishonour* (978-1-78463-089-8)

V.H. LESLIE
*Bodies of Water* (978-1-78463-071-3)

WYL MENMUIR
*The Many* (978-1-78463-048-5)

ALISON MOORE
*Death and the Seaside* (978-1-78463-069-0)

ANNA STOTHARD
*The Museum of Cathy* (978-1-78463-082-9)

STEPHANIE VICTOIRE
*The Other World, It Whispers* (978-1-78463-085-0)

ALSO AVAILABLE FROM SALT

ELIZABETH BAINES
*Too Many Magpies* (978-1-84471-721-7)
*The Birth Machine* (978-1-907773-02-0)

LESLEY GLAISTER
*Little Egypt* (978-1-907773-72-3)

ALISON MOORE
*The Lighthouse* (978-1-907773-17-4)
*The Pre-War House and Other Stories* (978-1-907773-50-1)
*He Wants* (978-1-907773-81-5)
*Death and the Seaside* (978-1-78463-069-0)

ALICE THOMPSON
*Justine* (978-1-78463-031-7)
*The Falconer* (978-1-78463-009-6)
*The Existential Detective* (978-1-78463-011-9)
*Burnt Island* (978-1-907773-48-8)
*The Book Collector* (978-1-78463-043-0)

RECENT FICTION FROM SALT

KERRY HADLEY-PRYCE
*The Black Country* (978-1-78463-034-8)

CHRISTINA JAMES
*The Crossing* (978-1-78463-041-6)

IAN PARKINSON
*The Beginning of the End* (978-1-78463-026-3)

CHRISTOPHER PRENDERGAST
*Septembers* (978-1-907773-78-5)

MATTHEW PRITCHARD
*Broken Arrow* (978-1-78463-040-9)

JONATHAN TAYLOR
*Melissa* (978-1-78463-035-5)

GUY WARE
*The Fat of Fed Beasts* (978-1-78463-024-9)

NEW BOOKS FROM SALT

XAN BROOKS
*The Clocks in This House All Tell Different Times*
(978-1-78463-093-5)

RON BUTLIN
*Billionaires' Banquet* (978-1-78463-100-0)

MICKEY J C ORRIGAN
*Project XX* (978-1-78463-097-3)

MARIE GAMESON
*The Giddy Career of Mr Gadd (deceased)*
(978-1-78463-118-5)

LESLEY GLAISTER
*The Squeeze* (978-1-78463-116-1)

NAOMI HAMILL
*How To Be a Kosovan Bride* (978-1-78463-095-9)

CHRISTINA JAMES
*Fair of Face* (978-1-78463-108-6)

This book has been typeset by
SALT PUBLISHING LIMITED
using Neacademia, a font designed by Sergei Egorov
for the Rosetta Type Foundry in the Czech Republic.
It is manufactured using Creamy 70gsm, a Forest
Stewardship Council™ certified paper from Stora Enso's
Anjala Mill in Finland. It was printed and bound by
Clays Limited in Bungay, Suffolk, Great Britain.

LONDON
GREAT BRITAIN
MMXIX